SHIFTER
Sensual
Captivity

AUBREY ROSS

ELLORA'S CAVE
ROMANTICA PUBLISHING

An Ellora's Cave Romantica Publication

www.ellorascave.com

Shifter

ISBN 9781419960994
ALL RIGHTS RESERVED.
Shifter Copyright © 2008 Aubrey Ross
Edited by Mary Moran.
Photography and cover art by Les Byerley.

This book printed in the U.S.A. by Jasmine–Jade Enterprises, LLC.

Electronic book publication July 2008
Trade paperback publication May 2010

This book is a work of fiction and any resemblance to persons, living or dead, or places, events or locales is purely coincidental. The characters are productions of the author's imagination and used fictitiously.

SHIFTER

∞

Prologue

ℬ

A shrill scream jarred Mal Ton from a dreamless sleep. He grabbed his pulse pistol off the rickety nightstand and opened the door with a mental command. Increasing the mutant intensity of his eyes, he illuminated the hallway as he ran. A second scream guided his steps. He rushed down a flight of stairs into the bowels of Fane's hideout.

Fane stood in a doorway halfway down the main corridor. He calmed his people with firm directives and unflagging patience, dispersing the crowd pressing in around him.

Mal Ton watched from the shadows, amazed at Fane's unshakable composure. People liked Fane. They sensed his strength of character and obeyed without question. Few leaders ever achieved this level of devotion.

Tucking his weapon into the back of his pants, Mal Ton approached his friend. "There's no imminent danger, I presume?"

Fane moved aside so Mal Ton could see into the small room. Sean Wylie sat on the floor beside the narrow bed with a young woman cradled in his arms. She trembled and tossed her head, babbling incoherently. Sean rocked her and brushed damp strands of hair back from her misshapen face.

"Her name is Sarah," Fane whispered. "She made the sacrifice. She's our most powerful dreamer."

The sacrifice. It was such an innocuous term. *Sarah allowed the Protarian lentavirus to ravage her body and mutate her mind.* That didn't sound nearly as civilized. Were prophetic dreams a fair exchange for physical well-being?

"What's her connection to Sean?" Mal Ton looked at her face, ignoring the impulse to avert his gaze. No one sought out the Underground until they had exhausted all other options. They were all mutants in one way or another.

"Sarah is Sean's younger sister."

She screamed again, thrashing and arching despite Sean's careful hold.

Mal Ton stepped back into the corridor. If there was no danger, there was no reason to linger.

"You're restless, my friend." Fane joined him in the hallway.

"We were created for action. Waiting will never sit well with me."

"I suspect you'll be back in action shortly. The accuracy of Sarah's dreams tends to determine their intensity."

Accepting the information with a nod, Mal Ton leaned against the cool stone wall. "Any word from Stilox?"

"Nothing new."

Though they had both been born on Stilox, only Mal Ton still considered it home. War with the Protarians had destroyed the planet, consigning Stilox survivors to scattered climate domes. Mal Ton couldn't look at Protaria's lush forests and elegant cities without remembering all the Stilox soldiers who had perished in the never-ending war. The Underground was better. Hidden in, and beneath, deserted sections of Protaria's capital city, Fane's sprawling hideout was home to mutants from a number of races. Still, Mal Ton longed for the scorched landscapes and twisted ruins of Stilox.

"Fane," Sean called. "She's ready now."

Fane stepped back into the bedroom while Mal Ton went no farther than the doorway. Sarah sat on the edge of her bed, hands folded in her lap. A scarf had been wrapped around her head, concealing everything but her glowing amber eyes.

"The human test subjects are in Old Towne." Her voice was well modulated and composed. No one would guess she had been writhing on the floor moments before.

"Old Towne is huge," Fane said. "Can you be more specific?"

Her gaze shifted to Mal Ton and apprehension inundated his empathic receptors. He stepped back into the hallway, unwilling to add to her discomfort.

"I saw an old-fashioned marquee. I'm pretty sure it was the Paramount Theater."

"Is there anything else?"

"You need to hurry. They aren't reacting well to captivity."

Chapter One

ೞ

"I have them, sir."

Mal Ton Adoha glanced up from his thermo scanner and turned his head toward Sean Wylie. "Send your signal to the main display."

Sean complied. His scanner zoomed in on a dilapidated structure directly ahead of their scout ship. The windows had been sealed and there were no visible signs of life. Luckily, their search didn't depend on visual clues. Seven life-form indicators blinked near the center of the scanner grid.

"Only four humans," Mal Ton muttered. "Damn."

"You didn't really think Max would keep them all in the same place, did you?"

"No," he grumbled. "He hasn't missed a trick." As if fighting the Protarians wasn't challenging enough, one of his own kind had turned traitor and sabotaged their efforts at every turn. Mal Ton searched the other buildings visible on the display. "Can you set down here?" He motioned toward the level rooftop directly across from their target.

"Structural integrity is acceptable but we're exposed from all sides."

"No one down here is going to approach a police scout ship. This sector has been condemned for years." The ship's external shield could be modulated, creating the illusion of any number of vessels. Invisibility had been the original goal of the technology. Still, clever distortions worked nearly as well.

"Any chance of snagging their surveillance feed?" Mal Ton asked. They would only get one shot at this. Once Max learned they were on to him, it would make any rescue attempt that much harder. "These scans aren't giving us much to go on."

Sean activated a holoconsole directly in front of him, allowing him to access several systems simultaneously. "There's nothing to jack. They've gone completely low-tech. I might be able to amplify their voices, but we'd do better with one of my bugs."

A smile quirked one corner of Mal Ton's mouth. Sean loved his tiny contraptions, spent hours improving and modifying the miniature, remote-controlled spies. "Send its signal to the main vidscreen."

Sean hooked the control strap over two of his fingers and adjusted the thin pad across his palm. His thumb animated the bug with smooth, almost imperceptible movements. He launched the device through one of the munitions tubes. The image bobbed and bumped as the bug zipped toward the shabby building. A warped window frame provided a gap big enough to facilitate the bug's insertion.

Water-stained walls and the dim glow of a portable light source filled the vidscreen. Mal Ton heard muffled voices but couldn't make out their words. A rhythmic hum pulsed through the transmission, lending a surreal quality to an otherwise gloomy scene. Presented from the perspective of Sean's newest invention, the image shifted and panned as the bug turned its tiny head.

"I've got to take a piss," one of the men announced. He pushed to his feet and ambled toward the door.

"Thanks for the update," one of his companions muttered. He was dressed in threadbare garments and his face was smudged with dirt. The unconventional uniform would help him blend in with their present surroundings.

"See if you can locate the women," Mal Ton suggested. According to their intel all the captives were female.

Sean maneuvered the bug along the perimeter wall and down one of two adjacent hallways. The first three rooms were snugly sealed, but Sean managed to slip the bug under the fourth door. Mal Ton caught a glimpse of a windowless cell before the bug abruptly ascended, causing the scene to blur.

"I *need* him, Lorelle." A slender blonde woman cried. Mal Ton's nanites allowed him to assimilate any language to which he'd been exposed. His recent interaction with humans had given him a rudimentary understanding of Earthish. "My head is pounding. If I move, my muscles cramp, but I can't stand still. I have to do this."

The blonde faced a dark-haired woman dressed in a khaki uniform. The insignia on her sleeve identified her as Protarian militia, but her ivory skin and the shape of her eyes assured him she was human. An odd sense of awareness stirred within Mal Ton as his gaze settled on her full-lipped mouth. Had he met this woman while he was on Earth? Surely he would have remembered someone so striking. Shaking away the disconcerting thought, he tried to assess the situation objectively.

The brunette finger-combed her hair out of her eyes and gestured toward the door. "Those bastards did this to us." Filled with compassion and fury, her gaze was more violet than blue. Unique yet familiar. Where had he seen her before? "Do you really think they give a damn how much we suffer?"

"He helped me before," the blonde argued. "You didn't see how bad it got. I can't go through that again. I'm not as strong as you are."

Three agitated steps took the blonde from one end of the room to the other. Two simple cots and a composite food tray were the cell's only furnishings. The blonde was alone with Lorelle, so where were the other two humans?

"He didn't cure you." Lorelle slipped her hands into her pants pockets and took a hesitant step toward the blonde. "The hunger came back. For all we know, giving in to him is what's making you sick. Maybe humans are incompatible with their... Oh my God, maybe this is why we were taken. They could be trying to impregnate us! You have to fight through the urgency, see if you can break the cycle for good."

"You don't understand. It gets worse each time. I have to have him now!"

Sean carefully maneuvered the bug out of the room and resumed his search for the other humans.

"It doesn't take much imagination to figure out what that was about." Sean's tone was heavy with frustration and regret. "Is she infected?"

"They both are," Mal Ton admitted. "The guards have been *treating* them."

"Why weren't they given the vaccine? This doesn't make sense."

Even if Mal Ton hadn't been able to understand their words, the symptoms were unmistakable. Anxiety, muscle cramps and sexual frenzy. If Max had infected these women intentionally, Mal Ton would— He needed to focus on the mission. Max would pay for all his wrongs, but rescuing the humans took top priority.

"I can't get into any of the other rooms." Sean sent the return code to the bug and deactivated its transmitter. "How do we proceed?"

"Get into position and wait for my signal."

"The blonde was pretty far gone. We better wait until after her next *treatment*. I'm not sure she'll make it back to headquarters if we don't."

Mal Ton tensed. He despised abuse in any form. Seduction had his whole-hearted support. He even stooped to deception from time to time. But this was different. Like a chemical addiction, the lentavirus created an uncontrollable urge, an artificial hunger that robbed its victim of choice.

"She has to have it, sir. The virus has seen to that." Though his tone was firm, compassion softened Sean's expression.

"If they harm her in any way, we move in."

"Understood." Sean unfastened his safety restraints and stood in the narrow aisle between the two seats. His eyes clouded then flashed with amber light. He spread his arms as visible particles of energy swirled around him, building in speed and intensity. The light expanded, encompassing his face and then his body. His corporeal form disintegrated, leaving only mist.

* * * * *

Lorelle pressed the back of her hand against Karla's forehead. "You're burning up." Carefully schooling her expression, Lorelle hid the dread twisting inside her. Had the other captives developed this bizarre illness? And how much longer could she ignore the burning inside her own body?

Karla moaned and tossed her head. Crossing her arms over her chest, she pressed her thighs together, shaking. The nature of her distress was more apparent with each movement. "Make it stop. Please make it stop."

"If you...relieve the pressure yourself, will that help?" She'd never felt so useless in her life. Fourteen years of military life hadn't prepared her for a sexual crisis. Karla was the youngest of the captives and her easygoing demeanor called to the protector in Lorelle.

"I've tried," Karla wailed. "Nothing works. I need Luke!"

Despite her determination to be difficult, Lorelle pounded the heel of her hand against the locked door. "Hello! Luke, get your ass in here!" She shouted in Standard. Even these imbeciles understood the intergalactic trade language. "We need your help now!"

The guards refused to reveal so much as their names, interacting with them as little as possible. So Lorelle had assigned them names, starting with the oldest and meanest. Matthew ignored them for the most part, delegating their care to Mark and Luke.

Luke burst into the room, weapon drawn. Mark was half a step behind. Taking up a defensive position in the doorway, Mark let Luke take the lead.

"What the hell is wrong with you?" Luke snapped. "You made it sound like someone was dying in here."

"What's wrong with her?" Lorelle indicated Karla with an angry sweep of her hand. "She's climbing the walls."

The men exchanged knowing glances but said nothing for a long, tense moment.

Luke took a step toward Karla and Mark caught him by the arm. "We can't."

"Will — *he* be angrier if we fuck her or if he returns to find her feral?"

"Who said anything about fucking her?" Lorelle wasn't as surprised as she sounded. Karla hadn't spelled out what happened on the ship, but Lorelle knew it had been sexual. "She needs a doctor."

"She needs our cum," Luke said bluntly. "The urgency will continue to escalate until she gets it."

Lorelle's stomach clenched and her chest burned. "How *convenient*." Wrapping her arm around Karla's shoulders, Lorelle offered what comfort she could. They'd been kidnapped, drugged and terrified. Without one word of explanation, they'd been taken from Earth and dumped in this slum. Scrubbing a hand over her face, she tried not to lose control.

Karla twisted out of Lorelle's hold and threw herself against Luke's chest.

Mark aimed his rifle at Karla's head and ordered, "Back off."

Driven by instinct as much as anger, Lorelle snatched Luke's pistol out of his hand and jump-kicked Mark's rifle. The weapon clattered against the far wall as Mark lunged for her. She spun around and kicked him in the head with all the force she could muster. He swayed then sank to one knee, clutching his head between his hands.

"This is pointless." Luke wrestled Karla's hand away from his crotch. "We haven't reported your outbursts because we knew you'd be disciplined. Is that what you want?"

Why would they care if she were disciplined? His vehemence made her pause. "I want my life back."

Karla sobbed, clutching the front of Luke's uniform with both hands. "Please. I can't wait." Her meaning easily transcended the language barrier.

Lorelle crept back, covering both men with the pistol. "Will fucking her make this stop?" Tension gripped her belly, spiraling down between her thighs. Where was Matthew? Why hadn't he responded to this ruckus?

"It doesn't matter." Mark managed to look at her, but his voice remained tight. "Luke already fucked her once. He can't risk it again and I'm tempted to let you both rot after that little stunt."

She deactivated the safety and aimed the gun at his face. "Answer the question."

"Yes. Fucking her will send the virus into remission—temporarily." Mark revealed each word with obvious reluctance. His eyes narrowed and he struggled back to his feet.

"Are you trying to get her pregnant?"

Her hostile gaze was fixed on Mark, but Luke replied, "I don't think we could get her pregnant even if we wanted to. Conception is a lot more complicated than what's going on right now."

"What happens if you fuck her more than once?"

"Some people absorb our—"

"It's forbidden." Mark shot Luke a scathing glare. "That's all she needs to know."

"We don't have a choice," Luke stressed, ignoring Mark's hostility.

Lorelle shook away the unanswered questions and focused on the crisis at hand. "Karla, are you sure this is what you want?"

Karla nodded. Tears streamed down her cheeks even as she rubbed against her captor. "I can't...I can't go on like this."

"This is not your fault," Lorelle insisted, terrified that she was watching a preview of her own fate. "You've done nothing wrong."

Luke took Karla's face between his hands and whispered into her ear. Karla didn't understand Standard, but it didn't seem to matter. Of their three captors, Luke allowed them the most dignity. It was Luke who had seen they had clean clothes and were allowed to shower.

Mark took a step forward. Lorelle waved him back with the gun. "You sit against the wall."

"She needs us both." Luke met her gaze, his expression tense and serious.

She glared at him without shifting the gun from Mark. "Why?"

"Each time the virus flares it takes more of the antigens to counteract the symptoms. I can't create a strong enough reaction alone."

Lorelle fought back a frustrated scream and clasped the gun with both hands. "Try. If it doesn't work—"

"It will only waste time she can't afford." The sexual frenzy had driven Karla beyond modesty. She boldly stroked the front of Luke's pants as she guided his hand to her breast. She pushed her fingers into his wavy hair and parted her lips for his kiss. Luke hesitated, obviously waiting for Mark.

"Where is Matthew?" Lorelle asked.

"He went outside," Mark told her. "It's now or never."

His smug smile made her finger flex against the trigger. She would die before she let these bastards touch her, but Karla had made her decision clear. She could always shoot Mark after...

"If you hurt her, I will kill you." Lorelle followed him with the gun as he crossed the room. She widened her stance, ready to act at the first sign of trouble. Restlessness crept over her in scorching waves. She needed to lie down, spread her legs wide and thrust her fingers into her throbbing pussy. Would a screaming orgasm push back this madness? Karla said it hadn't helped her. It didn't matter! There was no way she'd reveal weakness to the enemy.

Mark pulled Karla's shirt off over her head. Then Luke lifted her against him while Mark rid her of her pants. Her undergarments followed in quick succession and Lorelle had to look away. Murmurs and gasps teased her imagination. How would they take her? Did they secrete these antigens or was it a reaction within the victim's body?

"Why don't you join us?" Mark's deep, throaty tone made her insides clench.

"I'm not that desperate."

"Yet."

She shot him a quick glare and her wayward gaze lingered, refusing to budge from the erotic scene. Luke had turned Karla, bringing her back against his chest. He played with her breasts, firmly rolling her nipples. She arched her neck and angled her head, offering Luke her mouth. His tongue snaked out and traced her lips before delving inside.

Lorelle's lips tingled as she watched the consuming kiss. Their lips didn't quite meet and she could see their tongues sliding against each other. Mark knelt in front of Karla and bent his head toward her mound. Using only his tongue, he pushed into her slit and caressed her clit. Lorelle barely suppressed a moan as fire burst between her thighs. She wanted to be licked, needed— No! Not like this. Not with *them*.

Ruthlessly flicking his tongue against the tender bud, Mark drove Karla to a fast, hard orgasm. She tore her mouth away from Luke's and tangled her fingers in Mark's dark hair. "More! Fuck me with your fingers. Do it again."

Mark caught her clit between his thumb and forefinger and glared into her eyes. "Protarian men don't take orders from females." Luke caught her elbows and held her arms back while Mark plucked on the sensitive nub. Karla twisted and gasped, unable to escape his punishing caress.

Had he understood her words or just her tone? None of the guards had spoken in Earthish, but that didn't mean they couldn't. Lorelle shook away the possibility. Earth was new to intergalactic trade. There was no reason for these men to know their language.

"Be still," Luke directed. "Relax your thighs and accept your Master's touch."

Master? Was it just a figure of speech, or did these men dominate their lovers? Perspiration gathered between Lorelle's breasts. The room was chilly and dank, so why was she sweating?

Gradually Karla stopped fighting against the stimulation. Lorelle watched Mark's fingers pull and release Karla's clit much as Luke had done with her nipples. When she rested against Luke's chest and unclenched her thighs, Mark parted her folds with his thumbs and captured her clit between his lips. His cheeks worked as he carefully sucked on the sensitive nub. Karla cried out, shaking with another orgasm.

Lorelle's body rippled and clenched. Why was she watching this? They were obviously no threat to Karla. At least not physically.

"My turn," Luke said breathlessly. "I want her to ride my face so I can shove my tongue right up inside her."

"Get on with it," Lorelle snapped. "This is not a game."

"The concentration of antigens is determined by the level of our arousal," Mark explained, suddenly sounding more like a doctor than a soldier. "That includes her. The more turned-on she is, the stronger the reaction. Now stop distracting us."

Luke spread out on his back and guided Karla down on top of his face. She rocked back and forth, grinding her pussy against his mouth. Lorelle crept toward the doorway and checked the hall. How would Matthew react if he arrived in the middle of this display?

When she turned back around Mark was kneeling on the other side of Luke. He bent Karla forward. One hand held the back of her neck and the other was buried between her thighs. Lorelle couldn't see what Luke was doing, but Karla's cries told the story.

Mark raised his hand to his mouth and licked Karla's cream from his fingers while his gaze bore into Lorelle's. "You're next."

Her mind balked against the taunt, but her body burned even hotter.

Mark unfastened his pants and angled his body so Lorelle could see exactly what he was doing. He stroked his cock with one hand and carefully pulled on his balls with the other. His abdomen tensed and his eyelids drooped. He better not waste his seed when Karla was so desperate for it!

Focusing on her indignation, Lorelle fought back her response to the carnal tableau. Had the virus been engineered or was it naturally occurring? Were men affected by it or did it only make women sex-crazed animals?

A sharp cry drew her attention back to Karla. Luke squeezed her ass with both hands then scooted out from under her. "Good girl." With a passion-dark smile he moved in front of Karla and raised her torso so she was on her hands and knees. He pushed his pants past his hips and offered her his cock. Lorelle only got a glimpse of his erection before Karla sucked it into her mouth. There was nothing tentative or shy in her desire. She turned her head this way and that, taking as much of him as she could.

Lorelle's nipples rubbed against her bra with each agitated breath. Regardless of the reason for this exhibition, she had never seen anything so arousing. Mark stroked himself with one hand while he fucked Karla with the other. Lorelle watched his fingers slide between Karla's dusky folds and push into her core. Every thrust made Lorelle ache and throb. Karla's muffled cries and eager wiggles sent fresh waves of lust through Lorelle.

"Are you desperate yet, soldier girl?" Mark jeered. "Come over here. Brace yourself against my shoulders and I'll lick your pussy while I fuck your friend. Are those long legs flexible or just strong? Let's find out how wide you can spread them."

"Shut up!" She averted her face, knowing her flushed skin and dilated pupils were giving her away. The torment continued in her peripheral vision despite her determination to remain unaffected by the scene.

Karla raised her ass toward Mark as he prolonged her orgasm with his clever fingers. Were they really that good or was the virus making Karla ultra-responsive? Lorelle's pussy tightened painfully, craving even one of the orgasms Karla had enjoyed.

Mark guided his cock to Karla's entrance and buried himself to the balls with one hard thrust. She cried out around Luke, but it didn't disturb his steady rhythm. Like a moth drawn to a flame, Lorelle turned her head back around. Hooking his arms beneath Karla's elbows, Mark clasped his wrists at the small of her back and pinned her arms against her body. He pulled her away until only the tip of Luke's cock remained in her mouth.

Long, thick and shining with saliva, Luke poised within the circle of her lips. He took Karla's face between his hands and tilted her head back, his fingers tangling in her hair. Mark drew back too. They paused, teasing her with a hint of their fullness. Lorelle trembled. They held Karla as securely as any restraints, positioning her for the taking.

Lorelle had never been overpowered by a lover. She knew danger excited her, but her military career had prevented her from exploring the pleasures teasing her imagination.

Mark violently impaled Karla, filling her feminine passage as Luke shoved back into her mouth. Lorelle pressed her hand over her pounding heart. She had never seen anything so...savage, yet so beautiful. They moved in perfect synchronicity, Luke rocking in and out of Karla's mouth while Mark fucked her creamy cunt.

Swiping her forehead with her uniform sleeve, Lorelle focused on the wall directly in front of her. It didn't help. The slap of flesh against flesh combined with muffled cries of pleasure kept the image alive in her mind. Her body felt hollow and hot. She couldn't wait until they left so she could ease this ache!

Boot heels rang in the hallway outside the airless room. Damn it! Matthew was back. She turned toward the door, steadying the gun with both hands. Matthew threw the door wide and batted the pistol out of Lorelle's grasp as if she were no more than an irritant.

"*Resalnto!*"

"*Wer...orten...nottric...craa,*" Luke panted out in between deep thrusts.

"*Figal hastaminet ordentez—*"

"Explain that to her." Mark continued the rapid shuttle with his hips. "We refused to touch her until Lorelle pointed the gun at us."

Lorelle laughed. What a load of crap!

"How did she get a gun?" With a disgusted shake of his head, he turned his angry gaze on her. "Even if what he claims is true, how the hell am I supposed to convince my supervisor you forced them to fuck your friend?"

Luke cried out and buried himself in Karla's mouth. She bucked wildly and Mark drove deep one final time. He came with a strangled yell then released his hold on her arms. Karla shoved Luke back and wiggled away from Mark before either man could catch his breath.

"Are you all right?"

It was an odd question. Matthew generally showed no interest in their well-being. Still, Lorelle repeated it in Earthish so Karla could understand. The younger woman nodded and frantically gathered her discarded clothes. Accepting her assurance with a stiff nod, Matthew aimed his pulse pistol at Mark and pulled the trigger. Karla dove for cover with a startled yelp. Lorelle scrambled for the nearest weapon as Matthew turned his gun on Luke. When his comrades lay crumpled on the floor, Matthew returned his attention to Lorelle.

She crouched near the bunk, steadying her pistol with both hands. Amber light burned through the darkness in his eyes, casting his face into shadow. He seemed to shimmer around the edges then illumination burst through his skin. Lorelle shook. What the hell was this? A ripple began at his feet and swept up the length of his body, transforming his shape and sculpting his features.

He grew taller and broader. A supple brown vest accented his brawny arms and well-defined chest. Black pants of the same material hugged his lean hips and muscular thighs before disappearing into calf-high boots. His dark hair lengthened, becoming tiny dreadlocks that swept away from his face and fell to the middle of his back. Smooth, caramel-colored skin stretched over arrogant features. Unlike Matthew and the other guards, his skin tone was more gold than bronze. Was this man a different species or from a different region of this world? A short beard shadowed his jaw and authority emanated from his bearing.

Lorelle swallowed hard and focused on his eyes. The amber light faded leaving behind glistening teal. "Who are you?"

"There will be time for explanations later. Where are the other two humans?"

He hadn't refused to answer, just postponed her curiosity. He'd incapacitated the enemy, she wasn't about to argue with him. She pushed to her feet and tucked the pistol into the back of her pants. He watched the action in silent approval, waiting for her reply.

"The others were locked in a room across the hall, but we haven't seen them in several days." A shiver raced down her spine as a shadow separated itself from the wall. She took an automatic step back. "How many of you are there?"

The shadow darkened and solidified, becoming a man in the blink of an eye. Unlike the shapeshifter, this man materialized out of thin air. It was all Lorelle could do not to rub her eyes. The shadow-man was as light as the shifter was dark with burnished gold hair and a slightly tanned complexion. The ink-black center of his eyes receded, revealing pale green irises. Was he making himself appear more human or did the transformation indicate something she didn't understand?

"There are only two of us," the blond answered her nearly forgotten question. "That should be enough." He softened the boast with a playful wink.

"Move out." Expectation filled the shifter's tone.

Questions flooded Lorelle's mind. Knowing the shifter would be annoyed by any hesitation, she postponed the inevitable barrage.

"Don't you have shoes?" the blond asked as they moved into the corridor.

"Our possessions were discarded before we left Earth," Lorelle told him.

"We're not going far," the shifter said.

Lorelle kept Karla in front of her and watched for any sign of ambush. What had the shifter done with the real Matthew? She had so many questions.

A blast from the shifter's pistol opened the door Lorelle pointed out and they found the other two captives huddled in the back corner of the room.

"It's all right," Karla assured them in Earthish. "They're going to take us out of here."

A lump formed in Lorelle's throat as she heard Karla's words. She wanted to be rescued as badly as the others, but how could they be certain they were being rescued and not captured by a rival force?

Adrenaline had given her a momentary reprieve from the burning, but she knew it was just a matter of time before the virus reared its head again. She would never get through this unless she focused on one thing at a time.

The shifter hurried them through the building and up to the roof. A cool evening breeze caressed Lorelle's face and her curious gaze swept her surroundings. Crumbling buildings pressed in on all sides, decaying and forgotten. Yet in the distance a massive metropolis rose against the hazy sky. Why had this section of the city been abandoned?

"Let's go," the shifter prompted.

He pointed to the ship waiting on the adjacent building and Lorelle's heart fluttered with hope. This was real. They were being rescued! Nine humans had survived the crash along with two crewmembers. But they'd been divided into three small groups and taken to separate locations. Had these men located the others? As the shifter had said, there would be time for questions once they reached safety.

A daunting gap separated the two rooftops. On her best day she might be able to make the leap, but they'd been basically sedentary since leaving Earth. As if on cue, a hatch in the side of the ship opened and a ramp extended, providing a narrow walkway between the two buildings.

The blond man led the way. After crossing the ramp, he stood inside the hatch and helped each woman as she passed into the interior of the ship.

As Lorelle prepared to cross, the shifter proffered his hand. She accepted the assistance with a wan smile and his warm fingers enveloped hers. Damn the man was big! She gained her footing and he stepped onto the ramp behind her. A warm tingle spiraled from the nape of her neck to her nipples and on to the apex of her thighs. Was the virus flaring again or was she just attuned to him?

Needing a distraction, she nodded toward the crest on the side of the ship. "Are you law enforcement?"

"Something like that." He ducked through the hatch behind her and turned to retract the ramp.

The two men took their seats in the cockpit, leaving the women to secure themselves to the bench in back.

"Are we being arrested?" Karla's tone was shaky and uncertain.

"We've done nothing wrong," Lorelle stressed. "Why would they arrest us?"

"Did he kill those men?"

"I'm pretty sure they were just stunned." She had no idea why Karla would care one way or the other. In Lorelle's opinion, the guards' only value was the information they might have possessed. She'd hardly glanced at the fallen men after the shifter blasted them.

"Are you their leader?" the blond man asked, amusement sparkling in his gaze.

"I was just unfortunate enough to speak Standard," she explained.

The shifter's mouth curved in a subtle smile, but he didn't say a word.

The ship shuddered then banked sharply as they left the rooftop.

"Are the others being rescued as well?" They'd only been airborne a few moments when Lorelle lost the battle with her curiosity. "How did you know where to find us? Why were you looking? What planet is this and why were we taken from Earth?"

The blond swiveled to face her, flashing another breath-stealing smile. "I'm Sean Wylie, that's Commander Adoha, and this should answer the rest of your questions." He motioned toward the display across from them and Doctor Andrea Raynier's image came on screen.

"I'm sorry I can't be there in person to explain this," Andrea began, "but rest assured you're in capable hands."

The captives had realized Andrea was their common tie shortly after they were taken from Earth. Each had been a patient of Dr. Raynier's. Most had been treated for some form of infertility. Was Andrea responsible for their abduction or had she been abducted too?

Easily anticipating the question, Andrea's message went on. "I was abducted by the people of this star system. Our information is rather sketchy. We're not sure if you were abducted or if you volunteered for some fictitious scientific program. Regardless, we're certain you didn't intend to be shot out of the sky."

"Why isn't this interactive?" Lorelle asked, and Sean paused the message.

"An interactive transmission, regardless of how well it's encrypted, could reveal your location. Until all the captives have been recovered we're not taking any chances." He reactivated the vidscreen.

"Three factions are at war and we're caught right in the middle. The Protarians are the bad guys. We're pretty sure they're behind your abduction. The Stilox rebels have recently joined forces with the Mutant Underground." She rubbed the bridge of her nose and shook her head. "And then there's Max. He's one of the mutants, but he turned against the

Underground. He's the one who shot down your ship and has been holding you captive."

A soft, masculine chuckle sounded somewhere beyond the transceiver's range. "Focus, kitten," the man said in Standard. "Don't try and explain everything that's happened, just tell them what they need to know right now."

Kitten? Lorelle tensed at the endearment. Had Andrea been seduced by one of these offworlders? Were females intentionally infected so they could be more easily controlled? It wasn't the first time the possibility had crossed her mind.

"They need to know the truth." Andrea's gaze connected with the unseen man and obvious affection glowed in her expression. "I owe them that much at least." She shifted her attention back to the transmitter and continued in Earthish. "The Protarians used a biological weapon against the people of Stilox. The virus killed millions, as the Protarians intended, but the survivors developed a wide range of mutations. If you're hearing this message, you've encountered people with these mutations. We have a counteragent for the biological weapon. It restores the person's health. Unfortunately, it doesn't reverse the mutations."

"Hold on," Lorelle interrupted again. "Is this weapon what's making us sick? Can Andrea cure us?"

"Yes and yes," Sean said. "A vaccine has been available for years. We have no idea why the Protarians didn't inoculate you."

"Obviously they wanted us to develop these mutations and the other delightful side effects," Lorelle snapped, her pulse keeping time with her rising temper.

"The onset illness is extremely dangerous," the shifter said, not bothering to turn around. "Why would they abduct you and bring you to another planet just to watch you die? It's far more likely that Max screwed up their schedule when he shot down your ship. You'll all be treated as soon as we reach our destination."

"Treatment better not mean what it meant to…the guards." Lorelle felt the rapid rise and fall of her chest and knew she was breathing too fast. Heat bathed her skin like the midsummer sun, followed immediately by icy chill. Her teeth chattered and perspiration beaded on her brow. How much longer could she fight this?

Sean released his safety restraints and crossed the cabin. "How long have each of you been battling the symptoms?"

Lorelle quickly translated for the others.

"Karla has been sick the longest," she told Sean. "She was already infected when I was kidnapped. I'm not sure about the others. As near as I can figure we've been on this planet fifteen days."

"Are you the only one who hasn't had sex since leaving Earth?" He touched her face and she jerked away.

"I'm fine." His lightest touch sent prickly sensations dancing across her skin.

"Sure you are." He returned to his seat and spoke to Mal Ton in a hushed, urgent tone. Anything they said in their native language couldn't be good for her.

"Can you turn Andrea back on?" Lorelle desperately needed to think about anything other than the pressure building between her legs.

Sean reactivated the message, his worried gaze lingering on her face.

"Mal Ton is taking you to Fane. At the moment, that's the safest place for you. Fane is the leader of the Mutant Underground."

Mal Ton must be the shifter. Sean had introduced him as commander something-or-other. Why was Andrea so familiar with these aliens?

"Max is fighting Fane for control of the Underground. The Protarians want to combine selected mutations with…with the alteration I made to your DNA. We're not sure why Max shot down your ship. He might be negotiating with the Protarians or hoping to manipulate Fane. Both Max and the Protarians will fight like hell to get you back. But you don't need to be afraid. Fane's people will make sure nothing happens to you." She paused for a friendly smile and tucked a strand of hair behind her ear. "I'll come to you as soon as I can."

The screen went blank and Karla turned on Lorelle. "She kept saying 'us' and 'we'. Who is she aligned with, the Stilox or the Underground?"

"She said she'd altered our DNA," one of the other captives pointed out. "What did she mean?"

Barely able to think past the pounding in her head, Lorelle forced her mind to focus. Was it possible she was the only one who had figured it out? "You honestly don't know?"

Her question was met with a chorus of, "Know what?"

Looking at Karla, she asked, "How long ago did you participate in the RENA program?"

"Andrea transcribed my DNA for the second time nine years ago."

Most people had some sort of cosmetic alteration performed at least once a year. If Lorelle's security update hadn't required a complete DNA profile, she might still be wondering why she looked so young.

"Andrea ran the second sequence on me eighteen years ago," Lorelle admitted. "And according to my DNA profile, I haven't aged a day in all that time."

Chapter Two

ॐ

Daniel Keller paused outside Cassie's lab and smoothed down his hair. He adjusted the fall of his jacket, hoping the material hid his erection. All he had to do was think about her and blood filled his groin. The prospect of touching her, even brushing his hand against hers, left him achy and hot.

Only in his mind did he dare call her Cassie. To the world she was Doctor Cassandra Myer, innovative nanobiologist and — more importantly — favorite daughter of Chancellor Howyn, the most powerful man on Protaria. Keller had known her since childhood. They'd attended the same academies and belonged to the same social circles. She'd married one of his closest friends, dashing Keller's hopes of making her see him as more than an acquaintance.

Then the Stilox had killed her husband, leaving her alone if not emotionally available. Keller couldn't stop thinking about her, imagining how life would have been if she had chosen him instead of Nicho.

He spent hours each night indulging his fantasies, picturing her there with him, or better yet, beneath him. She'd whisper his name and wrap her long legs around his waist as he sank into her wet pussy. His cock bucked at the thought and he stifled a groan. He had to stop doing this to himself. She wasn't his to claim, no matter how many times he pictured them together.

He pressed his hand against the scanner, announcing his presence. Only those approved for entry could trigger the interrupt chime. Even then it was up to Doctor Myer whether or not to leave her work.

"Hi, Daniel," Cassie's voice revealed her surprise. She was the only one he knew who called him Daniel. Everyone else called him Keller or sir. "Father said you'd be offworld for at least a month."

"Recent developments necessitated my return. May I come in? I hate talking to the wall." He hated not seeing her velvet brown eyes and the enticing curve of her ass.

The door to the lab slid open and Keller walked in. The new facility was easily three times the size of the one it had replaced. Andrea Raynier was supposed to be working at Cassie's side, paving the way for the fulfillment of all their ambitions. Instead the stubborn human had empowered the Stilox rabble with far more than they were meant to know.

"What can I do for you?"

Now there was a question he'd love to answer honestly. *Kneel in front of me and suck me until I'm about ready to die then bend over the counter and let me fuck you up the ass.* How he loved that round little ass. It was such a contrast to her lush breasts and tiny waist.

He forced away the inappropriate thoughts and cleared his throat. "How do you like the new facility? Are you all settled in?"

"The new project Father assigned me is so complex I've hardly noticed the change." She rubbed the nape of her neck and strolled toward him. His pulse accelerated with each step she took. "Surely you didn't subject yourself to all this security just to ask how I liked the new lab."

He heaved an audible sigh and prepared himself for the performance of a lifetime. His black-market sources had failed him utterly and Cassie was the only one he knew who wasn't intimidated by the chancellor.

"There's been another outbreak in Old Towne. I promised I'd provide the treatment before it gets completely out of control—again."

"Why do they allow this to happen? All anyone has to do to be treated is register with—"

"They're suspicious and I don't blame them. People with mutations are treated like pariahs or they're manipulated and exploited. Believe me, I know."

Her gaze narrowed and she slipped her hands into the pockets of her lab coat. "You worked for my father long before your abilities manifested. It wasn't like he recruited you because of your mutation."

"This isn't about me. It's about a group of children who are struggling for their lives. We both know your father would rather pretend Old Towne is really abandoned, but I don't have that luxury. Grab a box of the counteragent off the shelf and I'll be on my way."

"There are other sources for the treatment. Why involve me?"

"Anyone I send to seek out one of those other sources is going to report back to your father and I sure as hell can't approach them myself. Who would be stupid enough to sell contraband to Chancellor Howyn's pet mutant?"

She glanced at the drug locker, her expression tense and conflicted. One more push and he'd have her.

"Everything in this lab is inventoried. How do I explain–"

"Synthesize a new batch," Keller suggested before she could change her mind. "All you'll have to do is delete the log entry. No one needs to know."

"Give me a couple hours," she relented with a sigh. "I'll have the package sent to you. *Do not* come back here. He might be my father, but that's not the advantage most people think."

* * * * *

Mal Ton set the ship down on a vacant lot a short time later. After modulating the external shield to make the ship appear derelict, he powered down the other systems. Lorelle's fierce expression lingered in his mind as his fingers flew over the control consol. He'd shoved his way into the room and she'd faced him down, her defiance blasting his empathic receptors. Her spirit intrigued him even more than her lovely features and pleasing form.

"Commander," Sean said sharply in Stilox. "Look at her eyes. She's turning feral."

Lorelle slumped against the bulkhead, the woman on either side struggling to keep her upright. She tossed her head and panted fast and shallow. Her eyes glowed, the vibrant purple shocking against her pale skin.

Once a victim turned feral, there was no help for them. They evolved into creatures so savage and animalistic soldiers agreed to kill each other rather than endure the transformation.

Mal Ton rushed to the passenger cabin, fear twisting through his chest. Releasing her restraints with a clatter, he swept her into his arms and activated the hatch with a well-placed kick. Her body emanated heat. Fire, frenzy, insatiable desire. As long as her symptoms progressed no further there was hope.

"Secure the ship and see to the others. This can't wait." Mal Ton ignored the women's concern and leapt to the ground, not waiting for the ramp to extend.

He hurried down the alley toward the back door to Fane's headquarters. Little of the Underground was actually underground. Fane had commandeered a series of abandoned buildings and connected them with passageways. Only the research facility was located beneath the city. All the other buildings were equipped with modulators similar to the one disguising the ship. Fane's people moved from one hideout to the next with no rhyme or reason, leaving each building vacant for random periods of time.

A guard scanned open the door as soon as he recognized Mal Ton. Skirting the great hall, Mal Ton descended the spiral stairs leading to the lower levels. Ostan looked up from his vidscreen as Mal Ton burst into the clinic.

"She was exposed to the Protarian lentavirus approximately fifteen days ago." He placed her on the examination table and the doctor hustled to his side to begin an assessment.

"She's human?" Ostan asked as the scanner initialized.

"Yes." Mal Ton reached beneath her, retrieved the pistol from the back of her pants and set it on a nearby counter.

"Did she have sexual interaction with any of the Protarians?"

"No."

Ostan gave her an injection then resumed his scan. "I presume she's one of the test subjects Max intercepted."

Mal Ton nodded, waiting for the doctor's plan of action.

After administering another injection, Ostan rubbed his pointed chin. Though his health had been stabilized by the counteragent, his mutated DNA resulted in permanent changes to his appearance. His forehead was unusually broad and the sharp angle of his cheeks made his face triangular. Pearlescent and fair, his skin provided a stark contrast for his ink-black eyes.

"Well?" Mal Ton prompted impatiently. She'd draped her forearm over her face as they entered the clinic. Light sensitivity often accompanied the fever. She lay lax and unresponsive except for her rapid breathing.

"How badly do you want to save her?"

"Isn't that your job?"

"Ethics prevent me from giving her what she needs. I can treat the fever and keep her from dehydrating, but…"

"Is she feral?" Mal Ton's mouth dried up, making each word an effort. So many had succumbed to the Scourge down through the years. He'd thought himself numb to the sorrow.

"She's close. There's still a chance you can bring her through this."

"A chance *I* can bring her through?"

Ostan narrowed his gaze on Mal Ton's face. "You know more about this illness than anyone and that includes me." Ostan handed him a cluster of injectors. "These will balance her electrolytes and keep her from lapsing into a coma. Keep her cool and make sure she doesn't hurt herself. It will take at least forty-eight hours for the counteragent to completely bind the virus. Until then there's nothing more I can do."

Mal Ton scooped her up in his arms and strode from the clinic. Old resentments clawed their way to the surface. This war had cost him so much, so many lives, so many wasted years. And still it demanded more.

He glanced at the woman nestled against his chest. She stirred restlessly, rotating toward him and wrapping one of her arms around his neck. A heated pang swept from his throat to the pit of his stomach. He tightened his grip, pressing her more firmly against his thundering heart.

"Where are we?" she rasped.

"This is Fane's headquarters. You're safe now."

She blinked repeatedly and raised her head. "Where's Karla?"

"You lost consciousness on the ship." Clasping Lorelle firmly in his arms, he took the stairs two at a time. He could feel desire gathering within her, seeping through the drug-induced calm. "The others are on their way to the clinic."

"Where are you taking me?"

He didn't bother with a reply. She'd figure it out soon enough and he wanted to be alone with her when she did. He reached the landing at the top of the stairs and rushed toward his bedroom. Slipping inside, he lowered her feet to the floor and triggered the lock with a mental command.

Lorelle twisted out of Mal Ton's grasp and took a quick step backward. "This isn't going to happen." Her legs wobbled beneath her. The instability heightened the spinning in her head. She faintly remembered being in a clinic, bright lights and beeping scanners. "Take me back to the clinic."

"It won't help. I think you know that."

"Sean said there was a cure."

He leaned against the door and crossed his arms over his chest. She was tall and athletic, yet he'd carried her like a child. She could hold her own with most human men. Her agility compensated for their strength. But Mal Ton wasn't human. Her gaze descended from his arresting features to the corded muscles in his arms and shoulders. If he was determined to fuck her, there was no way she could stop him.

Did she want to stop him? She'd been ready to blast her head off to end this…hunger.

"You were given the counteragent, but it needs time to bind the virus."

"I'll risk it." Despite her bravado, her senses began to burn.

He advanced without warning, crossing the room with three long strides. "Let's get one thing straight right now. This is and will always be your decision. I have no interest in rape. But I would rather not watch you die simply to appease your pride."

His hands clasped her upper arms and his scent teased her nose. It would be so easy to melt into his embrace, to part her lips and invite his kiss, to feel his cock pushing into her, stretching her, filling her…

She kept her gaze averted and concentrated on her breathing. "I've resisted this long. I can ride it out."

"Why put yourself through that?" He caressed her neck and trailed his fingertips along her jaw. His tone was as seductive as his touch. "If you're hungry you eat, even if the enemy provides the food."

She glanced into his eyes. "Are you the enemy?"

"You know I'm not."

With a sudden twist, she evaded his touch and took a step backward. "I know little more than your name."

"Andrea trusts me. Doesn't that account for something?"

His charming smile was anything but reassuring. She couldn't afford to like him. How could she fight off her yearnings when everything about him appealed to her?

"Which planet is this?" she asked, desperately needing a distraction. "Where is Andrea?"

"This is Protaria." Mal Ton clasped his hands behind his back, his vest stretching tight across his sculpted chest. "Andrea is on Stilox."

"Then the…mutants are Protarian?" She was uncomfortable with the word, though the mutants themselves had embraced it.

"You're just prolonging the inevitable."

"It is not inevitable. All I need to do is resist until the counteragent kicks in."

"You'll never last that long."

"I won't if you keep drawing my attention back to what I'm feeling," she snapped. Any surge in emotion caused heat to flare in her pussy. She had to remain calm. "Talk to me. Help keep my mind occupied."

He inclined his head, his gaze bright and assessing. "What would you like to know?"

"Anything. Just talk." She crossed her arms over her breasts, shocked by the sensitivity of her nipples. More annoying than a tingle and more intense than an itch, the sensation made her squirm. "How did the mutations begin?"

Shifter

"Andrea's message explained—"

"Tell me again."

He heaved a sigh then repeated the information. "After decimating our planet, the Protarians resorted to biological weapons in their attempt to obliterate our existence. Not only did we fail to die, we founded a civilization right under their noses."

"Then you're originally from Stilox?" She tried to put some distance between them. He countered her step for step, but compassion had softened the predatory gleam in his eyes.

"I am, but the Underground is populated with mutants from several different worlds."

"Who is the bigger threat, Max or the Protarians?"

"They each pose different dangers."

He stayed just out of reach, a constant temptation. "What's being done to find the other captives?"

"Everything in our power."

She raked her hair with both hands, annoyed as much by his appeal as his evasion. Keeping her gaze off him wasn't helping. She could *feel* him. She wanted to climb his tall body and feast from his lips. All she had to do was reach out and he would end her suffering.

"Are we finished talking?"

Her clothes rasped against her skin, damp and irritating. Why was she so damn hot? "I presume shapeshifting and...whatever you call what Sean did are not the only abilities available to you. How did you find us?"

"A seer narrowed your location to a couple of city blocks. Sean and I scanned each building until we found human bio signs."

"So we wait around until this seer senses where the others are being kept?"

"Why are you concerned with the other captives? You should be focusing on your recovery."

"I'm just curious about your resources," she muttered, risking a glance at his face. Big mistake. Desire leeched the strength from her knees and made her hands tremble. God, he was gorgeous. "If the seer fails, what's plan B?"

"We don't rely entirely on those with clairvoyance. Much of our intel is gathered the old-fashioned way."

"Spies and hackers? That sort of thing?" She swayed, reaching blindly for support while her ears started ringing.

"Enough of this foolishness." Mal Ton picked her up and tossed her facedown over his shoulder. Her breath whooshed out, cutting short her indignant cry. Instead of striding to the bed as she'd feared, he took her into the bathroom and turned on the shower. "Your temperature just spiked. We have to cool you down or your brain will fry."

How the hell did he know what her temperature was? He placed her beside the shower and pinned her against the wall with one hand. She tried to hit him, but his long arm kept his body out of reach. Before her muddled brain could remember she had legs, he'd kicked off his boots and pushed her beneath the cool spray, blocking her retreat with his body.

"That's cold!" She pressed herself against the far wall, trying to avoid the water.

"It's tepid. You're feverish."

He continued to undress with alarming speed, so she grabbed the handles, debating which way to turn. With the water still streaming over her body, she didn't want to scald herself. Before she could choose, he stepped up behind her and dragged her hands away from the controls. Her pulse raced and fire erupted between her thighs. If she was feverish, why could she feel heat emanating off him?

"I'm not going to fuck you!" She couldn't look at him, didn't trust her reaction. "Why can't the doctor inject me with whatever is in your... There has to be a *medical* treatment for this."

"The antigen can't be synthesized." He turned her around, his hands lingering on her shoulders. He didn't speak again until she looked into his eyes. "Scientists have been studying the phenomenon for decades. Unless the antigen is passed directly from one body to another while both are sexually aroused, it has no effect on the virus."

"That's ridiculous." But Mark had insisted the strength of the transfer was determined by Karla's arousal. It was either true or a well-rehearsed lie used to justify their lechery. "Who would engineer this into a biological weapon? It doesn't make sense."

"They wanted it spread quickly among the adult population. It makes perfect sense."

He started unfastening her uniform top and she grasped his wrists, water streaming over her face and down her body. "Fucking doesn't spread the virus, it puts it into remission."

Returning his hands to her shoulders, he leaned in and brushed the crest of her cheek with his lips. "The longer we wait, the wilder you'll become."

"Afraid you won't be able to control me?" She regretted the question as soon as she heard the challenge in her tone.

"Do you want me to control you?"

"I want to understand why this is necessary." It wasn't a lie, but it wasn't accurate either. The thought of being controlled by Mal Ton teased her imagination and fueled the inferno building inside her. She'd never had a lover willing, or able, to physically dominate her.

"The initial contagion is inhaled, but the virus can only survive for a matter of minutes in its airborne state. Once it's absorbed by a host, they remain contagious indefinitely. However, it's much harder to pass the virus from person to person."

"So they included a sexual stimulant to ensure the virus would spread?" After the initial shock of the water passed, she was able to relax a bit.

41

"It's not just the stimulant. When people improve after having sex, it seems logical to repeat the 'treatment'."

She shuddered, appalled by the ruthless design. "People fuck each other, thinking they're providing a cure when in reality they're spreading the infection? And the compulsion comes back regardless of how many people... Who the hell came up with this?"

"I'll give you a detailed history once you're past this crisis."

"The guard said pregnancy isn't a risk. Was he telling the truth?"

"Yes. Having sex with me won't give you little alien babies." One corner of his mouth formed a sardonic smile and a fresh rush of heat assailed her system.

"Will Karla and the others need more of the antigen?"

He shook his head and wrapped his fingers around the nape of her neck. "They're safe. And so are you."

She wanted to believe him, but it was only partly true. She wouldn't be safe until she allowed him to give her the antigen. Gazing into his eyes, the temptation took root and swept through her in a languid wave. "How were we infected? Did someone do this to us intentionally?"

"I'd rather do this while you're still rational. We're running out of time." He tried to pull her closer. She shoved against his chest. "Are you a virgin? Is that why you're so resistant?"

"I am not a virgin, but I generally know a man for more than an hour before I have sex with him."

One of his brows arched in silent challenge. "You've never been tempted to indulge your fantasies?"

"What would you know about my fantasies?"

He responded with action instead of words. His long arms wrapped around her and his mouth settled over hers. Lorelle balled her hands into fists, clinging to the last few fibers of her stubborn nature. It felt wonderful to be held. Another fiber snapped. His lips were warm and patient. He teased and caressed when she'd expected force.

"Open your mouth," he whispered against her damp lips.

Hard and hot, his body enveloped her. He pushed his knee between her thighs, pulling her hips forward until his erection aligned with her belly. Her mound rubbed against the unyielding muscle in his leg, compounding the ache already pulsing there.

Her startled gasp allowed him to deepen the kiss. His tongue eased past her lips and his fingers tangled in her hair. Tension coiled. Her legs trembled and reality spun away. She'd been taken from her homeworld without explanation, much less permission. Now she was expected to yield her body as well?

With a frantic tug, she freed her mouth from his sensual assault. "I won't do this! I can fight the urge for a few more hours."

"Lorelle," he framed her face with his hands and stared into her eyes, "in a few more hours you'll be feral. Your DNA will recode and there's no cure once that transformation begins. I understand your need to resist. No warrior wants to surrender, but you are still in control. I will not rape you. I'm asking you to let me ease your pain."

Her body shook. Never in her life had she lost a battle, there had been occasional retreats, but never a surrender. "If I say no?"

"I'll do what I can to minimize your suffering."

Her heart lurched and she glanced away. "I…don't want to die."

"I know." He stroked her jaw with his knuckles, his voice soft and low. "Say the word and we'll fight this thing together."

Mal Ton watched the rapid rise and fall of her breasts. The conflict emanating from her was nearly as intense as the heat. She kept her face turned away, yet her nipples formed distinct peaks beneath the wet material. He admired her determination. Still, they'd postponed this as long as they dared. He was about to repeat the directive when she pulled her top over her head and handed it to him. She looked so forlorn, it was all he could do not to crush her to his chest and stroke her hair. All the tenderness in the world wouldn't save her right now. Tenderness? When had he ever been tempted by tenderness?

He tossed the soggy top over the shower partition and it landed with wet splat. She still wouldn't look at him, so he glanced at her naked breasts. High and round, the firm mounds would fill his palms. Her nipples were deeply flushed and tightly erect.

She drew in a deep, shaky breath and her breasts quivered. "If I find out this wasn't necessary…"

Grasping her chin, he tilted her head until their gazes locked. "I'm not going to hurt you. Some people actually enjoy this."

"I've accepted that it needs to be done, but I have no intention of enjoying it."

He laughed and pulled her arms behind her back. "That, sweetheart, sounds like a challenge. And I love a good challenge." She wiggled and twisted as he loosened her pants and pushed them past her hips. Her halfhearted struggle assisted him more than she realized. Soon her soggy pants joined her shirt on the other side of the shower stall.

Mutant fire stung his eyes as he gazed at her trembling body. Long, lean legs flared to gently rounded hips. He skimmed over her pussy. Once he allowed his gaze to linger there, he would be hard-pressed to look anywhere else. Her waist was trim and he would never tire of her breasts.

His cock twitched and his balls tingled. Everything about her was exotic and arousing. From the ivory pallor of her skin to the unusual color of her eyes, she was...alien. Only her dark, wavy hair could have belonged to a Stilox female.

"What's wrong?" Her hushed question drew his gaze back to her face.

"You're absolutely stunning." He covered her mouth with his, pleased to find her lips pliant if not yet responsive. After stroking the silken interior for several moments, he sucked her tongue into his mouth. She yelped and jerked back. "Are you always so skittish?" Her defiance gusted through him, yet he sensed a core of vulnerability. She might be a well-trained soldier, but she was still frightened and overwhelmed.

Guiding her hands to his shoulders, he leaned in close. "You kiss me this time. I promise I'll behave."

She pushed to the balls of her feet and fit her mouth over his. He didn't rush her, didn't attempt to take control. Her exploration began tentatively. She traced the shape of his lips with the tip of her tongue, her breath warm and teasing. By the time she delved inside, he was ravenous. She curled her tongue around his and he fought back a groan. Encouraged by her response, he forced himself to relax and let her set the pace.

Her skin was hot, not passion-flushed but feverish. He wanted to take her to his bed, to stretch out beside her and explore her curvaceous body at his leisure. No matter how appealing he found the idea, he couldn't risk it until her fever broke. Reaching behind her without separating their mouths, he decreased the water pressure to a cool drizzle.

She wrapped her arms around him, pressing her soft breasts against his chest. His hands ran up and down her back, cupping her bottom as he rubbed against her belly. Needing stability and leverage, he backed her against the wall. Her shoulders connected with the tiles and he took the kiss deeper.

Keeping their lower bodies flush, he eased his hand between them and cupped her breast. Just as he knew it would, the warm mound fit perfectly in his palm. He didn't want to forfeit the sweetness of their kisses, but her nipple begged for attention. She rested her head against the wall and arched, obviously anxious for the first touch of his mouth.

Her nipples gathered into pebble-hard points. He brushed his thumb over one and then the other. Her eyes drifted shut as he bent his head and caught one tight crest between his lips. He'd only meant to suckle for a moment and then move on, but her skin was intoxicating.

He caressed her bottom and the back of her thighs while his mouth continued to suckle. Her fingers closed around his dreadlocks, pressing him close, then pushing him away. The battle was not yet won. She had accepted the inevitability, but that would never be enough. He wouldn't be satisfied until she abandoned herself to the pleasure. He ignored her indecision and savored the delectable rasp of her nipple against his tongue.

His knee nudged her legs apart and he covered her mound with his fingers. She tensed but didn't try to stop him. Amplified by her fever, her pussy radiated heat. He wanted to lift her, wrap her legs around his waist and feel her hot cunt envelop his shaft. But he wanted more from her. He wanted more *for* her. Keeping her pressed against the wall, he knelt and grasped her hips. Her bush was neatly trimmed, offering a teasing glimpse of her feminine folds.

"Make room for my hand." Her thighs flexed then she moved her legs apart. He traced her slit with his middle finger, teasing without parting her delicate flesh. She rocked her hips and grasped his shoulders, needful murmurs escaping her throat. "If you want more, show me."

Her fingernails bit into his skin. Why was she still fighting? He could sense her need, feel the urgency pounding through her. *She doesn't know you. She has no reason to trust you.*

He was about to reassure her when she canted her hips and relaxed her thighs. His finger slipped between her folds and he groaned. She was already creamy. Unable to resist the temptation, he pushed into her core. Her inner muscles gripped him firmly. With a swirl of his wrist, he added a second finger, pulling nearly out before driving back in.

"Oh!" She arched into his next thrust. The forceful motion jostled her breasts. "God, that feels good."

Pumping steadily with his hand, he inhaled her tantalizing scent. The musky tang made him wild, made him eager to taste the slick cream coating his fingers. He kissed her belly and caressed her with his breath then parted her outer lips and exposed her tender clit.

The tiny nub was already swollen. She was so wonderfully responsive. He circled her with the tip of his tongue then caught the delicate hood between his lips. Her passage contracted with every gentle pull. He drove his fingers deep and flicked his tongue across the sensitive cluster of nerves.

She cried out, her pussy squeezing hard as she came. He prolonged the spasms with his mouth and slowly drew his fingers out.

"Let me taste you, *really* taste you. Do you like that?" It was so unlike him to ask. He generally took what he wanted with enough intensity to convince his lovers they wanted it too. Lorelle was different. He didn't want her stiff with resignation. He wanted her writhing and begging for more.

Her violet gaze smoldered as she looked around the crowded shower stall. "How?"

His grin was unabashedly sexual. Draping one of her legs over his shoulder, he pressed his lips to her slit. With long, thorough licks and careful little nibbles he soon had her rocking against his mouth. She rolled her head back and forth, her fingers curved around the back of his head. Her scent filled his nose and her essence coated his tongue, evocative and addictive. Pushing up into the very heart of her, he savored her softness and her heat.

Another orgasm built within her. Gathering speed and force, the contractions curled around his tongue. She gasped, shaking uncontrollably as her pleasure saturated his empathic receptors.

Before the last spasm receded, he shot to his feet and found her entrance with the head of his cock. Her leg slid across his shoulder and down his arm, her knee neatly hooking his elbow. Her cunt surrounded him, wet and hot, yet incredibly tight. He gritted his teeth as he fought off the urge to ram his full length inside her.

"We can't...do it like this," she ground out in a strangled whisper. "I'm too heavy."

He hid his smile against her hair. She'd tensed so suddenly he was afraid he'd hurt her. "We'll be fine, sweetheart. I'm stronger than I look."

Chapter Three

ജ

Mal Ton was stronger than he looked? As if that were possible. Lorelle wanted to laugh. She had never seen muscles so starkly defined or a body so well conditioned. He lifted her and guided her other leg into place around his waist. His arms supported her effortlessly as his cock surged into her pussy. Deeper and deeper he stretched her passage until her abdomen ached.

She'd waited so long and needed this so badly, she whimpered from the sheer pleasure of being filled. Her fingers clutched his broad shoulders, feeling the subtle flex beneath her palms. Hot, hard male, he held her spellbound, vacillating between ecstasy and fear.

His groin pressed against her mound and he shifted her weight. "Lock your ankles behind me and hold on tight."

She hooked one foot over the other, her thighs hugging his sides. He grasped her bottom with both hands and anchored her against him. Tilting his head to the side, he took her mouth in a consuming kiss. His shaft throbbed in time with his heartbeat while his tongue moved in her mouth.

Relaxing against him, she caressed his tongue with hers and savored the fullness he created. He squeezed her bottom, his long fingers insinuating themselves between her cheeks. She murmured, unsure if she was encouraging his exploration or protesting the subtle invasion.

He pulled her hips away from the wall, allowing his long middle finger to reach its destination. Lightly teasing her anus, he circled the sensitive opening without venturing inside. She gasped and wiggled, each movement accenting his penetration.

"Be still." He nipped her chin. "Feel me."

She chuckled. "As if I could feel anything else."

His brow arched then he pushed his finger into her ass. "There are always more intense sensations. Never forget that." He repositioned his hand and thrust deeper. "Squeeze me. Squeeze me hard."

Resting her head against the wall, she tightened her inner muscles. He'd obliterated the hollow ache she'd endured for the past fifteen days and created an entirely new sort of urgency. Stroking the delicate membrane separating his finger from his cock, he sent sensations ricocheting through her abdomen.

"Harder," he coached. "I'm not going to move until you come."

She shook her head. "I can't come like this."

"Sure you can. Each time you squeeze, your clit is pressed against me. Imagine my fingers rubbing or better yet my tongue."

He held her close, the heat of his body a sharp contrast to the cool tiles. She clenched and her core tingled. A harder squeeze brought a stronger response. She rolled the pressure up the length of her passage and heard his appreciative groan. Her body bathed him in hot cream, encouraging him to move. He grew harder with each new squeeze, increasing the pressure on her clit.

She came with a sharp gasp, her core tightening rhythmically. When the last ripple passed, he slid his hands to the back of her knees and spread her legs wide. Her ankles unhooked and she braced herself against his shoulders.

He pulled back, pausing with just his cock head inside her. "Open your eyes."

She hadn't realized she'd closed them until she heard the throaty command. Raising her lids, she looked into his eyes. Amber fire caressed her face as he pushed back in, filling her, claiming her. *Mine.* Was it just his possessive expression, or had she actually heard the word?

He adjusted his stance and repeated the cycle, pulling out slowly and thrusting in fast. Her legs draped his arms and his forceful strokes pinned her to the wall. Amazed at her own resilience, she felt another orgasm build.

"I'm not ready to let you go." He punctuated the statement with an especially deep thrust.

Could he feel her pussy throbbing, or was it something more?

Pleasure burned away her speculation. She cried out and arched into his final thrust. He threw back his head and bared his teeth as he released his seed deep inside her. She wrapped herself around him and pressed her face into the bend of his neck.

Sizzling heat flowed through her veins, warming her entire body. Their harsh breathing echoed off the tiles and reality intruded. How long would it take for the antigen to ease this burning?

Stunned by his shattering orgasm, Mal Ton clutched Lorelle to his chest and waited for the world to refocus. His legs shook and tension gripped his back. He needed to reach the bedroom before he collapsed. He turned off the shower and stumbled out of the stall. She clung to him, her breathing erratic. Had they waited too long?

"Look at me."

Her gaze was bright, yet no more luminous than it had been on the ship. He triggered his optical scanner and checked her body temperature. It was still slightly elevated, though much improved.

He ran his hands up and down her back, pausing to squeeze her bottom. She felt so damn good in his arms. He couldn't distinguish her yearnings from his. Had the antigens had any affect on the virus?

"Why are you still hard? I felt you come," she whispered against his throat. "And I'm still restless as hell."

"Sometimes it takes more than once," he lied. There should have been a marked improvement.

He set her on the edge of the bed and slowly drew out of her snug heat. Not only was he still hard, he was hugely erect, the veins on his shaft boldly distended. Her gaze gravitated toward his cock, so he quickly turned her around, positioning her on her hands and knees.

The combined proof of their pleasure coated her folds and smeared her inner thighs. Would she be shocked if he licked her? Some people were put off by such things. His dominant nature stirred. He wanted his scent coating her skin and his taste fresh on her tongue.

He pushed two fingers into her core, marveling at her softness. She looked back at him, her eyes wide and curious. Raising his hand to his mouth, he sucked their essence from his fingers.

"We taste good together," he told her, watching closely for her reaction.

Her tongue brushed over her lower lip and desire inundated his empathic receptors. The essence of their passion lingered in his mouth. He wanted more than one teasing taste. Swallowing with difficulty, he pressed his face against her bottom and swirled his tongue between her folds. She gasped and lifted her hips, offering him better access to her cunt.

Drawing her with him as he rose, he splayed his fingers across the back of her head and cupped her mound with the other hand. "Taste me. Taste us."

Her lips were parted and waiting for him. He circled her clit while he kissed her and she bombarded him with hunger, demanding and raw. She rolled her hips, encouraging his caress with a throaty murmur. He reveled in the intoxicating slide of tongue against tongue. Gods, he could live on her cream.

"More," she whispered against his lips. "Please," she added when he tensed.

Heat assailed him along with a darker, savage need. Hers or his? He honestly couldn't tell. He brought his cream-slick fingers to her mouth and she eagerly suckled.

Desire exploded inside him, demanding his obedience. He wanted to pin her to the bed and fuck her mouth. Just the thought sent pleasure spiraling through him. Even if she would willingly offer her mouth, her arousal needed to be as powerful as his. Later, there was always later.

Shaking away the tantalizing image, he pulled her closer to the edge of the bed. She bent forward again and lowered her shoulders, bracing herself with her forearms. Her hips raised, the invitation unmistakable. Still he hesitated. Why were his urges so violent? He'd never been this close to losing control.

His gaze focused on her puckered little anus, displayed so temptingly. He wanted her unconditional surrender. She would moan and tremble as her body stretched to accommodate him. No! She wasn't ready to take him like that. She'd felt incredibly tight around his finger. He didn't even have a lubricant to ease his way.

He sucked in a long, steady breath. They had the rest of their lives to explore mutual pleasures. A fist grabbed his heart and squeezed mercilessly. Even in his desire-addled state he knew the thought was outrageous. She had been brought here against her will. She would likely leave at the first opportunity.

Tormented by the possibility, he bent toward her waiting body and inhaled deep. He needed her scent imprinted on his brain, yet he couldn't explain the compulsion. It was elemental and undeniable. He caressed her folds and circled her vaginal opening, all the while breathing in her scent.

Mine.

His touch settled over her clit, one finger on either side. Her bottom clenched and she murmured against the bedspread as he escalated her arousal. Moving closer, he licked from her clit to her star-shaped opening. She pushed up against him, surprising him with her acceptance. Had their first joining only stoked the flames?

He licked her again and again, never lingering in one place for long. She wiggled and moaned, trying to bring his tongue where she needed it most. Gathering cream from her pussy, he coated her anus and his dark nature roared. With firm pressure, he pushed his middle finger past the stubborn collar and into her smoldering passage. She gasped. He sighed. This would have to be enough for now. He worked his finger in and out, imagining how she would feel around his cock.

"Have you ever been fucked here?" He knew the answer, but his aching erection demanded he ask.

She shook her head and tightened reflexively. "Is that what you want?"

"Gods yes, but not right now." He dragged his finger out and they both shivered. "Do you feel any better?"

"No." She remained as she was, submissive and waiting. "I need — more."

He smiled. It was a subtle reprimand. Guiding his cock to her pussy, he slowly pushed inside. Her silken flesh embraced him, surrounding him with welcoming heat. He grasped her hips and established a steady tempo, deep and smooth. Tangling her fingers in the bedspread, she pushed into each firm down stroke.

She was so incredibly hot. He tossed his head and sped his movements. Mutant energy shot along his spine and forked out across the back of his head. Gasping, he gritted his teeth and fought back the shift. What was wrong with him? He hadn't spontaneously shifted in decades.

He sensed her urgency, her fear and desperation. Primal emotions surged, rolling across his empathic receptors and triggering a response just as savage in him. The abyss loomed, hungry, threatening to wrest her from his life.

He thrust faster, refusing to surrender. She writhed beneath him and arched into him, lost in passion's fury. He sank into her mind, shielding her from the darkness. Twisting and bucking, she came in distinct spasms while he wrestled with the abyss.

Buzzing filled his ears and mutant heat burned his eyes. *I will not lose her!* Flames engulfed him and he screamed. The sound echoed in his mind. The abyss groaned, folding in on itself, leaving him alone with the fire.

Searing heat exploded within Lorelle. The sensation began as an orgasm but catapulted her far beyond anything she'd experienced before. Mal Ton held her down, building the intensity with each forceful thrust. He was inside her mind! His mental penetration more invasive than his pounding cock. She screamed, no longer able to distinguish pleasure from pain.

He wrapped his arm around her hips and shuddered against her back. She felt him come deep inside her, his seed scalding its way to her womb.

The fire sputtered out and he slipped from her mind. She felt his absence with aching clarity. What had just happened? Trembling and dazed, it took all her strength just to roll them to their sides. If her legs hadn't been folded beneath her, she would have been trapped by his weight.

His arm lay lax across her hip. Uncertainty rippled through her. "Mal Ton?"

Silence.

She wiggled away from him, groaning as his cock slipped free. Turning to face him, she froze. He rested on his side, still as death. His eyes were closed and his face was void of expression. Her gaze flew to his chest as her fingers pressed against the side of his throat. The steady rise and fall was echoed by a subtle throb beneath her fingertips. At least she hadn't killed him! She released a shaky sigh and shook his shoulder. His skin radiated heat and he didn't react to the stimuli.

What had she done to him?

Dread cast its shadow upon her, making her insides quiver. She scrambled off the bed and threw open compartments until she found his clothes. Not pausing to fully dress, she struggled into the oversized shirt as she ran for the door. She hit the manual trigger, but nothing happened. Balling her hands into fists, she pounded on the locked portal.

"Help! Can anyone hear me? We need a doctor in here." No one responded and her anxiety mounted. She ran back to the bed, narrowing her focus to Mal Ton and nothing else. His forehead felt even hotter than his shoulder. He was much too big to drag to the bathroom, but there had to be something she could do. She grabbed her uniform top off the bathroom floor and wet it with cool water. Draping the damp material over his body, she tried the door again. "Hello! I need help in here—now!"

The door vibrated then released with a sudden pop. A dark-haired woman shoved past her and rushed to the bed. She took one look at Mal Ton and ran back to the doorway, shouting in a sharp burst of words Lorelle didn't understand.

"He needs a doctor," Lorelle said in Standard.

The woman's dark gaze swept over Lorelle, accusation clear in her sneer. "What did you do to him?"

"Nothing." *At least nothing intentional*, she clarified silently.

"If he dies, you die!" The woman lunged for her. Lorelle easily sidestepped the clumsy attack.

"Renée," a deep male voice drew Lorelle's attention to the doorway. "Go get Ostan." Though his tone remained conversational, warning flashed in his light green eyes.

The brunette obeyed without hesitation and Lorelle stared at the man. Dressed in black pants and a hip-length tunic that reflected their barbaric surroundings, he emanated power despite his lean build. Was this Fane? Dark hair brushed his shoulders, the front section pulled back away from his face.

"I didn't intentionally hurt him," she felt compelled to explain.

"I know." With a rolling stride, he crossed the room and checked Mal Ton. "How long has he been unconscious?"

"Just a few minutes. Why wouldn't the door open?"

"The locks are triggered by telepathic energy." He lit several candles in the branched sconce bedside the bed. The wavering light revealed hints of red in his dark hair, yet cast his angular features into high relief. "I'm Fane."

She didn't get the opportunity to return the introduction. A second man entered a moment later, carrying a small case. He acknowledged her with a stiff nod and her memory stirred. Had he been in the clinic when she first arrived? His hair was also red, but a garish, orange shade that contrasted sharply with his pale skin. He set the case on the bed beside Mal Ton and retrieved a handheld scanner.

"*Ducat prin taral form ra*?" Renée asked from the doorway.

Pain detonated behind Lorelle's eyes and crawled up the front of her skull. She clutched her head and closed her eyes as blood rushed through her ears. *What did she do to him*? Renée's words had sounded foreign, yet Lorelle understood their meaning.

"Why were you loitering in the hallway outside his door?" Fane countered in the same language.

"I was going to let him know I'd returned." Her dark gaze darted between Fane and Lorelle, her posture stiff and agitated.

"He has made his feelings clear. Back off. That's an order."

Her nostrils flared and she glared at Lorelle before she turned and walked away.

"He's trapped between shifts," the doctor told Fane. "I gave him an inhibitor to slow down the transformation. That way we can take action once his body decides which form to take. If he turns feral... Stubborn fool. He must have snatched her back from the very brink."

Should she tell them she could understand them? She crossed her arms over her chest and assessed the situation. Fane was incredibly hard to read. The doctor seemed almost sad. Why should she reveal a potential advantage? *To figure out how the hell it happened,* her rational side argued.

"Did Mal Ton shapeshift before he slipped into unconsciousness?" Fane asked her in Standard.

She swallowed hard. Mal Ton had been behind her, holding her down while he thrust his massive cock into her pussy. "I don't think so." She wasn't sure what had happened.

"Did his eyes turn gold?" Ostan asked.

Sex had never embarrassed her before. Why was she being so squeamish? "He was...behind me. I couldn't see his eyes."

The doctor approached her with the scanner. "Your fever is down. That's wonderful. Have your other symptoms eased?"

She glanced at Mal Ton and tension gripped her belly. "Did I infect him?"

"Not in the way you mean," Ostan assured her. "He was infected by, and treated for, the lentavirus long before he had sex with you."

"His ability to shift is responsible for his condition," Fane added, the hint of a smile curving his lips.

"May I take some samples? Understanding how your interaction with Mal Ton affected you might help me treat him. It's painless."

"Of course."

He retrieved several wand-shaped objects from his case and pressed the first against the side of her neck. "Are you having any new symptoms?"

She licked her lips, feeling very much like a lab rat. "I can understand you."

He tilted his head and lowered the second wand, which he had been about to fill. "You were not able to speak Standard before?"

"When Renée asked Fane what I'd done, I felt like my brain caught on fire. Then I just knew what she'd said. I don't know what language you were speaking, but I know what the words mean."

"Mal Ton has a language interface," Fane mused, "but how would she have—"

"Shouldn't we figure out how to wake him up?" She finger-combed her hair away from her face as the doctor finished collecting his samples. How could they just stand here while Mal Ton struggled for his life? Had Mal Ton known what he was risking when he decided to treat her? She'd resented his determination, felt as if he were exploiting her condition.

"His body must cycle through the shift," Ostan said, putting everything back inside his case. "There's not much more we can do."

She almost accepted the explanation until the doctor looked at Fane. There was a wealth of communication in his expression. They were deceiving her or protecting her or—she wasn't sure what.

"What aren't you telling me?"

"When Mal Ton shapeshifts he samples the DNA of the form he intends to take. You were in the process of transforming when he scanned you."

The pain in Fane's eyes explained what his words left out. "He's becoming what he saved me from."

"Possibly," the doctor said. "He might still be able to—"

"Can I cure him the same way he cured me?"

"You're not strong enough." Regret tinged Fane's tone.

"So we just let him die?"

"We?" Fane challenged. "What's your interest in his well-being?"

"How can you ask me that? He just saved my life."

"So you feel honor-bound to return the favor?"

She didn't understand the amusement in his eyes. There was nothing in the present situation that could be construed as funny. "Do you want him to die?"

"He is more important than you could possibly understand. I will do everything in my power to ensure his survival."

Ostan cleared his throat. "Sir, don't attempt anything until his body has had time to rebuild its energy stores. His levels are severely depleted."

"Of course."

"If his condition deteriorates, send for me immediately."

Fane nodded and the doctor left them alone with Mal Ton.

"Are you hungry? You've been through a lot in the past few hours."

"I've been through a lot in the past few weeks, but you're evading the issue. What needs to be done to revive Mal Ton?"

He smiled and her heart turned over in her chest. The expression rolled ten years off his face and made his eyes sparkle. Had he suffered a recent trauma or had life in the Underground simply taken its toll on his appearance?

"You're a woman of action, I take it?"

"The military does that to you."

"Fair enough." He clasped his hands behind his back and gazed into her eyes. "When Mal Ton sampled your DNA you were starting to transform. It will take an incredible amount of control to force back the transformation. He'll need energy and he'll need you."

"You said I'm not strong enough."

"You're not." He paused. "But I am."

"You're going to fuck Mal Ton?"

"No. I'm going to fuck you while you fuck Mal Ton."

Chapter Four

෨

Chancellor Howyn slammed into Keller's office with all the subtlety of a supernova. "What are you doing here?" he demanded, his face florid and blotchy.

"I work here." Keller folded his hands on his desktop and looked pointedly at the security transmitter. Every room in the chancellor's headquarters was monitored continually. Howyn should know better.

Aligning his body to block both of their faces, the chancellor waited for Keller to deactivate the audio feed before he went on. "I told you to stay offworld until I sent for you." He placed his fingertips on the edge of the desk and leaned toward Keller. "Pretty straightforward instructions, yet here you sit."

"Many of my responsibilities can be handled from a remote location. Some require personal attention. Do you want your lost package recovered or not?"

"Do you finally have a lead?" Howyn straightened his back and jerked on the hem of his jacket. Thank the gods his temper cooled as quickly as it flared.

"I might."

"Spare me your word games. I'm not in the mood."

"I've yet to determine the value of the new information, but I'm cautiously optimistic."

"You returned ahead of schedule for 'cautiously optimistic'?"

Keller kept his expression bland and carefully schooled his tone. "I should know more in a couple of hours." He was so fucking tired of pacifying this windbag.

The chancellor scowled, his beady eyes all but disappearing in his weathered face. "Run down your lead, boy. And check black-market sources for the counteragent. Whoever intercepted my package should have their hands full right about now."

"I don't understand, sir."

"Why doesn't that surprise me?" Howyn grunted his derision. "Our visitors were scheduled for inoculation upon their arrival. If they aren't given the counteragent soon, your current mission will be pointless."

"Why weren't they inoculated?"

Howyn glared at him. "I don't need to explain myself to you."

"The onset illness alone could —"

"We aren't having this conversation *here*. I gave you another possible lead. Get busy. It never hurts to have options. If Cassandra comes through for me though, your mission won't matter one way or the other." He left as abruptly as he'd entered.

Keller shoved his chair back and stood. Cassie again. She didn't intentionally devalue his accomplishments, but her creative mind frequently provided her father with alternatives at the worst possible moment. No matter which path Keller chose, Cassie arrived two steps ahead of him.

Cassie.

He despised her as much as he desired her. She did nothing to attract his attention. Still, he couldn't banish her from his mind.

He was a mutant, Chancellor Howyn's pet mutant to be exact. She would never see him as anything else.

If Cassandra comes through for me though, it won't matter one way or the other. The chancellor's dismissive words helped clear Keller's mind. What could she possibly do that would render the humans irrelevant?

* * * * *

Lorelle stared at Fane then snapped her gaping mouth shut. She had always appreciated candor. Still, his bold statement sent her imagination reeling.

"I've shocked you." One corner of his mouth quirked and his gaze sparkled. Was he imagining the act he'd mentioned so casually? Had he and Mal Ton shared women before?

"Do you people do anything but fuck?" Her voice sounded breathless.

"The body produces massive amounts of energy during the release of any strong emotion. Would you rather be angry or terrified, or feel sexual pleasure?"

She'd never thought of herself as a prude, but she was starting to suspect her experience would be considered limited in this star system.

"I'd rather find a different way of ending this crisis." She rolled up the trailing sleeves of her borrowed shirt, needing something to do with her hands.

"As would I. Unfortunately, I'm a realist. Mal Ton doesn't just need energy, he needs—"

"Does he need a female or is there something special about me?"

That knowing smile returned. "You are definitely special."

"I wasn't fishing for compliments. I meant—"

"I know what you meant." He took one of the chairs situated in front of the small desk and moved it beside the bed. "You're confusing what's happening to him with your reaction to the virus. They are related, but not the same. He'll sleep for hours. You should rest as well."

"None of the women I arrived with speak Standard. I should see how they're doing."

"Dressed like that?" He chuckled.

She glanced down at her bare legs then higher. Her nipples were clearly outlined by the shirt. How could she have forgotten her near nakedness? She felt comfortable with Fane. It didn't make sense, but she was completely at ease with him.

"Sean is downloading your language and the others are sleeping."

"Downloading it from where? Earth hasn't registered with any of the…" He started laughing and she didn't bother finishing the objection.

"Are you always this obstinate?"

"No." She looked away before he could see her smile. "I wasn't *just* being difficult. How is Sean going to download Earthish?"

"From Andrea of course."

"She's here?"

"I didn't say that."

"Okay, you lost me. Is he going to Stilox?"

"I didn't say that either."

Despite his relaxed manner, he didn't trust her. She accepted the evasion with a nod. If the situation were reversed, she wouldn't trust him either.

"Go take a shower then get some rest."

It wasn't a suggestion this time. She went into the bathroom and kicked aside her uniform bottom. The top was still covering Mal Ton. She refused to think about what had happened the first time she'd been in this shower. But her body didn't need the permission of her mind. Her pussy ripened and her nipples tingled. She had never imagined such pleasure was possible.

She removed Mal Ton's shirt and stepped into the shower stall. As warm water saturated her hair, her thoughts turned inward. Grief and rebellion had driven her into the military, but she soon found the vocation suited her. Life was regimented and disciplined, orderly and logical. She followed detailed procedures and successfully completed missions. She never realized how comforting she found the structure until it had been taken away. After shampooing her hair and soaping her body, Lorelle let the spray soothe her tense muscles.

"Are you doing all right?"

She blinked the water out of her eyes and glanced toward the door. Fane had only opened it far enough to let his voice carry. "I'm fine. How's Mal Ton?"

"Sleeping, like you should be."

"I'll be with you shortly, *sir*."

"Mal Ton's the one who likes to be saluted. I take a more cooperative approach to leadership."

"I'll keep that in mind."

"Here's a clean shirt. Anything particular you'd like to eat?"

Unbidden, the image of Mal Ton's magnificent body flashed through her mind. Fane made a noise suspiciously like a muffled laugh. She gasped. "Can you read my mind?"

"That image required no reading. I'll teach you how to shield your thoughts."

He eased the door shut and she let the spray cool her face. Was Mal Ton telepathic too? She thought back on how effortlessly he had anticipated her needs. No one was that perceptive without some form of paranormal help.

Drying with the semi-dirty shirt, she pulled the clean one over her head. This one covered her from neck to knees, but knowing Fane could read her mind made her feel naked. There was no mirror above the sink and she couldn't find a brush or a comb. She didn't know much about dreadlocks, but apparently they were wash and go. How did he shave? His beard was short and decorative, not the sort that grew naturally. At least on a human.

"You're stalling," Fane called through the door.

Crossing her arms over her chest, she abandoned her momentary refuge. "How telepathic are you?"

"Telepathy refers to the ability to send and receive thoughts." He sat in the chair with his feet propped on the side of the bed, crossed at the ankle. "Is that what you want to know?"

"What's the proper word for what you do?"

He grinned. "I do many things."

"You said you didn't need to read my mind to see that image. Does that mean you can read my mind if you want to?"

"Reading minds is not as advantageous as you'd think. Most of what goes on inside a person's mind is annoying babble."

"I'll take that as a yes." He'd moved Mal Ton to one side of the bed and covered his lower body with a sheet. Her uniform top was nowhere in sight. She laid the back of her hand across Mal Ton's forehead and frowned. "He's still really hot."

"So I gathered from your desire to eat him."

She didn't take the bait. "Should we be worried about his fever?"

"His condition is stable and will remain so until the inhibitor wears off or we intentionally wake him."

"What happens then?"

"I fuck you while—"

"Sorry I asked. If I choose not to cooperate, what happens to him?"

"There's a slight chance he can control the transformation, but it's far more likely he'll turn feral and I'll have to kill him."

"But that's what he said about the virus. You said this isn't caused by the virus."

"He is mirroring your symptoms because you had started to turn when he sampled your DNA."

"Why the hell did he sample my DNA?"

"I don't think he did it intentionally. He either lost control or saw no other way to force you into remission."

Her heart sank. "Anyway you phrase it, I did this to him."

"He knew what he was doing and he knew the risks."

That's what she'd been dreading most. It made her resentment so callous. She'd honestly thought Mal Ton just wanted to fuck her.

Someone knocked on the door and Fane jumped up to answer. She sat on the edge of the bed and studied Mal Ton's face. His lips were slightly parted, their shape sensual yet masculine. Everything about him was sensually masculine. She stroked his cheek with the backs of his fingers, enjoying the contrast between smooth skin and coarse beard. She owed this man her life. She wouldn't be able to live with herself if she let him die in her place.

A wide-toothed comb came into her peripheral vision, snapping her from her troubled thoughts. She took it from Fane's outstretched hand with an amazed smile. "Thank you."

"Comb out your hair then eat something—other than Mal Ton." He dragged the chair back where he'd gotten it and pulled out the other for her use.

She crossed to the desk and looked at the tray of food. Nothing looked familiar or particularly appetizing. "I don't suppose you have coffee?" Pulling her hair over one shoulder, she went to work on the tangled mass.

"I don't know what coffee is, so I'm afraid not."

"Damn." She plopped into her chair with an exaggerated sigh. "Only I could get kidnapped by aliens and end up on a planet without coffee."

They ate in companionable silence, or rather, she nibbled and he watched her. The dark blue beverage was light and fruity despite its unusual color. It had a pleasant effervescence that tickled her nose.

"How long were you in the military?" he asked as she pushed the tray aside and carried the tall glass of juice back to the bed with her.

"Technically I'm still in the military. But the answer is fourteen years."

"What is your role or expertise?"

"I do many things." She smiled behind her glass. It felt good to be the evader for a change.

"Do you have a mate?"

"Will you reconsider the course of action if I do?"

"No."

"Then why ask?"

He shrugged. "You were a patient of Andrea's. What was your affliction?"

"Infertility."

"How did recoding your genetics result in your immortality?"

"I'm not immortal." She rubbed the bridge of her nose and scooted back against the wall. What was left of the juice sloshed in the bottom of the glass. "I'm aging so slowly it's undetectable. That doesn't protect me from alien viruses or weapons fire."

He stared at her expectantly and the hairs on the back of her neck bristled. Heat spread from her belly outward, making her feel...fuzzy. She looked at the blue juice suspiciously. "What did you put in this?"

"There is nothing *in* it. Bental juice is naturally sedating." He rescued the glass from her hand as she slumped against the wall. "You obviously needed help relaxing." Setting the glass aside, he pulled her down across the bed and arranged her arms at her sides. "It will wear off in a little while. Now go to sleep."

* * * * *

When Lorelle woke she was curled against Mal Ton's side, enveloped by his warmth and wrapped in his strong arms. Nothing had ever felt so natural, so right. Her logical mind balked at the contentment, but it made no difference to her heart. She savored the peaceful lethargy. Moments like these were far too precious and fleeting.

Most of the candles had sputtered out, leaving the room in shadow. The mutants had spaceships and computers, but relied on candlelight? She didn't understand the contradiction. There was a lot about this place she didn't understand.

Her head rested on his shoulder and her fingers splayed across his chest. She stroked the impressive slope of one pectoral and then the other. Were all Stilox males naturally smooth? She grinned at the irrelevant thought and propped herself on her elbow so she could see him more clearly.

His features were relaxed and peaceful. Without his fierce stare, he didn't seem nearly so intimidating, yet he was every bit as appealing. How long did she have before Fane returned? There was so much she wanted to know, so much she needed to tell them. But Mal Ton's recovery had to come first.

A guilty smile parted her lips as her mind twisted the phrase. If her short experience with Mal Ton were any indication, she would come first. She would come over and over…but Mal Ton wasn't in control, Fane was. Would Fane be as concerned with her pleasure as Mal Ton had been, or would he be focused entirely on saving his friend?

She didn't have long to wait for her answers. Fane entered a few minutes later with a cloth bag tucked under one arm. He smiled at her and closed the door. She heard the lock activate and realized he'd triggered it with his mind. What else could he do with the power of thought? In most societies the strongest were chosen as leaders and Fane led people like Sean. His abilities must be amazing.

"Did you sleep well?"

"How long was I out?"

"Not as long as I would have liked. I'd hoped to get some things ready while you were sleeping."

She scooted to the edge of the bed and swung her feet over the side. "That sounds ominous."

"It doesn't need to be." He set the bundle on the floor and moved one of the chairs to the middle of the room. "It all depends on how we approach this. I'm gathering from your hesitation that humans are primarily a monogamist society."

"That's a sweeping generalization, but for the most part it's true."

"For the purpose of this discussion, we'll stick with what is generally accepted. What is the human attitude regarding sex?"

She shook her head. "That's much harder to define. Some humans treat sex like a recreational sport while others consider it the ultimate expression of love."

"How do you perceive it?"

"Somewhere in the middle." What utter crap. Excluding Mal Ton, she'd never had sex with anyone she didn't know well and care about deeply. She was far more comfortable kicking ass than making love, so her affairs had been few and far between. "My occupation has made sexual relationships complicated. I've—"

"Sexual relationships? Do you have to be in a relationship with someone to enjoy fucking them?"

She licked her lips and thought about Mal Ton. How much of what she'd experienced with him had been the virus and how much elemental attraction? Death had been a better choice than the guards, yet she'd felt a connection to Mal Ton the moment he revealed his true form.

"That's how it has worked for me in the past," she admitted.

"The virus is in remission. Are you still attracted to Mal Ton?"

"Definitely."

After a short pause he asked, "Are you attracted to me?"

She knew where this was leading. She glanced at the bed then tucked her hair behind her ear. Could she really fuck them both?

He smiled and rested his hands on the back of the chair. "I find you extremely attractive, but I would be willing to do this even if I didn't. Mal Ton is important to me and he's important to our cause."

There was a wealth of meaning in his tone. She couldn't decipher all the emotions gleaming in his gaze, but it was a glimpse into the darker, more intense side of Fane's psyche. "Are you…intimate with Mal Ton?"

"We aren't lovers if that's what you mean. There have been times when we exchanged energy and the most potent transfer of energy is obtained during sexual release. This is where our species differs from yours. There are occasions when fucking has nothing to do with our intimate relationships. And there are situations that necessitate the joining of more than two bodies. This will be like a blood transfusion, only much more fun."

She looked at him objectively. At one time he had been handsome. Hints of his appeal still lingered, but his eyes were too big for his face and his cheeks were painfully hollow. "Have you…?" How did you ask someone why they looked malnourished?

"If it weren't for Andrea Raynier I'd be dead," he answered her half-formed question. "Each day I grow stronger but I'm still recovering."

"I'm sorry."

He laughed and pushed the chair out of the way. "You're sorry I survived?"

"I'm sorry I come from a society that puts so much emphasis on physical appearance. You've been kind to me and you're loyal. You've put me at ease since you walked into the room. You're incredibly easy to talk to. These are all wonderful qualities."

"But we don't need to talk." He advanced with obvious purpose, his gaze fixed on her mouth. "We need to fuck. And your responses can't be faked or we're wasting our time. Is that going to be a problem for you?"

"I don't think so."

Grasping her by the upper arms, he pulled her to her feet. "I say we find out." He framed her face with his hands and pressed his lips over hers. She wrapped her arms around his back and closed her eyes. He smelled clean and faintly spicy, like incense or aftershave. His mouth was warm, the kiss firm yet patient. She opened for him, waiting for the slide of his tongue.

Mal Ton tossed restlessly, muttering in his sleep.

"Your bond is strong." Fane stepped back and lowered his hands. "We better restrain him now."

"Why does he need to be restrained?"

"Because I'm about to fuck his mate."

"His *what*?"

He ignored her outburst and retrieved wrist cuffs from inside the bag. "Don't be frightened if he growls. I won't let him hurt you."

Her heart lurched at the possibility. A snarling, out-of-control Mal Ton wasn't something she wanted to face without a pulse pistol. She couldn't see Fane's face, but she detected no amusement in his tone. Was he intentionally upsetting her? Emotions equaled energy and Mal Ton needed energy.

Fane walked to the far side of the bed. "Help me scoot him into the middle." Mal Ton twisted away from Fane. "Move closer to the bed. He'll follow your scent."

I'm about to fuck his mate. Fane's words echoed through her mind. She wasn't anyone's mate! Yet Mal Ton followed her like a beacon, rolling up onto his side as she neared. Oh, this wasn't good.

Fane closed the restraint around one of Mal Ton's wrists then passed it behind a stout pipe before securing the other cuff. Mal Ton's arms were extended above his head and the sheet rode low on his hips. Already she detected the bulge of his rising erection.

Returning to her side of the bed, Fane pulled her into his arms. "The inhibitor is starting to wear off. We need to get started."

There was an urgency in his movements that hadn't been there before. His mouth sealed over hers while their tongues danced. Her heartbeat sped and her feminine core melted. She clutched his back, pleased to find a firm layer of muscle. He wasn't nearly as weak as she'd first thought.

He separated from her long enough to discard his tunic then pulled the chair closer to the bed. His torso rippled, his abdomen tight and defined. When combined with his ultra-lean body, his angular features took on a menacing allure. He looked…dangerous.

Noticing her heated stare, he grinned. "There was a time, not too long ago, when I could have taken on Mal Ton." He sat down and held out his hand. "Come here."

Her anxiety grew with each step. Finding him physically attractive did nothing to soothe her nerves. If she allowed his touch out of obligation to Mal Ton, the sacrifice was selfless and noble. Wanting them both just made her wanton! And she could no longer blame her behavior on the virus.

He insinuated one knee between her legs and then the other, pulling her down to straddle his thighs. "Should I put my shirt back on? You seemed far more comfortable when you thought I was frail and personable."

The gentle mockery in his tone was unmistakable. She had completely misjudged him and he found it amusing. His warm hands slid up her legs and under her shirt, coming to rest on her hips. Her position put their faces on a level and she stared into his eyes.

"This isn't something you can passively accept," he told her. "We need your passion, your abandon, your primal energy. It can't be done *to* you. You must be an active participant. Do you understand?"

She nodded.

"Then take off your shirt."

With a deep, calming breath, she pulled the shirt off over her head and let it fall to the floor. His gaze swept from her face to her breasts, descended to her sex then returned to her face.

"You have a beautiful body to match your beautiful face." A sexy smile parted his lips. "Do you touch yourself?"

She licked her lips and averted her gaze. "Everyone touches themselves. When I'm on a mission that's often the only way I can get release."

"Do you use some sort of aid or just your fingers?"

He could only embarrass her if she let him. "I have a vibrator."

"Do you crave fullness or just clitoral stimulation?"

"Are we going to talk or fuck?" She reached between their bodies and covered the bulge in his pants with her hand. "It feels like you're ready to me."

"I've been ready since I first saw you. My inhibitions are not the obstacle."

She guided his hand to her breast. "Talking will make me more inhibited. I've always been more comfortable with action."

He grasped the back of her neck and pulled her face to his, ending the conversation with a demanding kiss. His other hand squeezed her breast, his thumb teasing the nipple. She stroked his chest and shoulders, sifting his soft hair through her fingers.

"Grab my knees," he whispered against her lips.

She reached behind her and found his knees, arching her back in the process. His legs moved apart and hers spread right along with them. Her bottom started to slip between his thighs, so she locked her elbows.

"Perfect." He caught her nipple between his teeth and laved the very tip with his tongue. One hand pressed against the small of her back while the other traced her slit. "Nothing is softer than a wet pussy. Nothing more evocative."

His fingers caressed her folds while his thumb rubbed her outer lips. Her body came alive, melting and relaxing as he gently stroked her. He circled her entrance, focusing her attention on the ache gathering there. Her clit tingled, protesting its neglect. She dropped her head back on her shoulders and rotated her hips.

"Be still. Let the sensations build."

Mal Ton's restlessness grew in tandem with her arousal. Fane pushed his fingers into her core and she whimpered, her inner muscles quivering around him. He circled her clit with his thumb and Mal Ton growled. Sensations sprang up deep inside her — heat, tension and expectancy. Fane pulled out and moved his wet fingers to her clit, leaving her passage hollow and throbbing.

She gripped his knees, desperate to move, craving the tingling pleasure hovering just out of reach.

"Not yet." He took his hand away and she hissed out a breath. "Coming now would be a waste of energy." He lifted her off his lap and motioned to the chair. "Kneel down and rest your forearms on the seat."

"Are you going to spank me?" She hadn't meant the question to sound quite so hopeful.

"Do you want me to?"

Her pussy twitched and she quickly looked away. "I was joking."

"No you weren't. Has anyone ever spanked you before?"

"We don't have time for this."

"Unfortunately you're right."

She knelt and bent over the seat of the chair. There was no doubt why he wanted her in this position. Tension gripped her abdomen, radiating out from her pussy and down her legs. She looked at Mal Ton while Fane dug in his goodie bag. Her body had just barely contained Mal Ton's cock. How in the world was she going to take them both?

Fane knelt behind her, his hand stroking her ass. "I'll do everything I can to make this easier, but I won't lie to you. If you've never done this before, it's going to sting."

Fabulous! Fear crawled down her spine and lodged in her stomach.

He moved her hair to one side and pressed a kiss to the nape of her neck. "I didn't mean to frighten you."

"It's probably better if I have realistic expectations."

Working his way downward, he rubbed her back and brushed her skin with his lips. She closed her eyes and concentrated on the soothing caresses, refusing to think too far ahead. His hand reached her bottom and he traced her crack, reaching between her thighs to tease her pussy. He parted her cheeks with one hand and found her opening with the other. Something pushed against her anus then slipped inside. The pressure was minimal.

"What is that?" She caned her neck but couldn't see exactly what he was doing.

"Just lubricant. Relax."

A warm gush filled her back passage and she gripped the chair. It felt so much like a man coming that her body spontaneously squeezed the applicator. He slowly withdrew the tube and tingles trailed in his wake. That hadn't hurt at all.

He entered her with his finger, his way eased by the lube. It felt odd yet enticing, a forbidden pleasure.

As his finger slid in and out, he reached around with the other hand and teased her clit. Her pussy clenched in on itself, accenting the penetration of his finger. She arched up to meet him helplessly as pleasure rushed toward climax.

"Not yet," he said again, and withdrew. The sensation sputtered out and she growled in protest.

He pulled her to her feet and kicked the chair aside, drawing her back against his chest. Tangling his hand in her hair, he guided her head to the side. Why was he being so aggressive? His lips urged hers open and his tongue pushed into her mouth. All hesitation evaporated in a flash flame of desire. He held her face with one hand while his tongue explored.

Dazed by the sudden change in his demeanor, she could do little more than return the kiss. A snarl escaped Mal Ton. She could hear him thrashing, but Fane wouldn't release her. He caressed her boldly, cupping her breasts and stroking her belly.

"Mine." Mal Ton's tone was so distorted she hardly recognized his voice.

With a sudden jerk, she turned her face toward the bed. Mal Ton lay on his back, the sheet twisted around one calf. His hands were balled into fists and his gaze burned with mutant fire. He pumped his hips, drawing her attention to his cock.

"We're going to have to be a creative," Fane whispered. "If I fuck you now, he'll tear the pipe right out of the wall."

Why had Fane waited so long? She kept the criticism to herself and asked, "What should we do?"

"Are you wet enough to get him inside you?"

"I think so."

"Then give him what he wants."

She placed her hand on Fane's upper arm and Mal Ton roared. "How will you control him if you're not inside me?" The bed shook with the violence of Mal Ton's struggle.

"I'll find a way." He pushed her toward the bed. "Touch him. Kiss him. *Soothe* him."

Mal Ton's struggle subsided somewhat as she crawled onto the bed. Her pulse throbbed in her ears. He wanted her, needed her so badly just the promise of fulfillment calmed him. She ran her hands up his thighs and he arched into the caress. Fascinated by his uninhibited reaction, she wrapped her fingers around his thick shaft. He shuddered, his chest heaving. Had he been this big before?

Moving with stealthy caution, Fane touched the back of her leg. *Make room for my hand.* Fane's voice sounded within her mind. *I want to make sure you're ready.*

She bent forward and circled Mal Ton with her tongue, shifting her position in one smooth movement. Mal Ton squeezed his eyes shut as she sucked him into her mouth. She recognized the salty, sharp taste. Passion, pleasure, fulfillment. Fane touched her gently. His fingers slid over her slick flesh and circled her clit.

We only get one shot at this. Don't let him come in your mouth.

Pulling back slowly, she sucked on the very tip before letting him slip from her mouth. He huffed and bucked, demanding more. She swung her leg over and straddled his hips, rubbing her sex against his cock.

"Mine." The word became a demanding litany as he repeated it over and over.

Lean forward and give him your breasts while I establish a link.

She wasn't sure what that meant, but she rested her hands on either side of Mal Ton's face and brought her breast near his mouth. He reared up and latched on to her with enough force to make her gasp.

Fane pushed his fingers into her pussy, thrusting carefully until her passage fluttered. His thumb brushed over her clit and she jerked.

Can you come without making a sound? I don't want him to realize I'm touching you.

She stroked Mal Ton's face, careful to match her gasps to the movements of his mouth. Fane thrust faster and pushed deeper, his thumb finally giving her what she needed. The pleasure was heightened by the possibility of discovery.

Her orgasm unfurled with gradual intensity. She clenched her teeth and embraced the pleasure, internalizing each deep spasm. A blazing pulse shot from Fane's fingertips and sped up her spine. The sensation lodged in the back of her head like a grappling hook. She made a needful sound, part cry and part whimper.

Mal Ton's eyes flew open and he released her nipple. Before he could analyze the reason for her incongruous behavior, she pushed up and guided his cock to her entrance. He felt massive and hot in her hand. Would all this fit inside her?

The mattress dipped subtly as Fane joined them on the bed. Mal Ton didn't seem to notice. She stared into his burning gaze and lowered herself onto his shaft. Centimeter by blissful centimeter she took him into her body.

Fane pressed against her back and cupped her breasts. Mal Ton snarled and tossed his head then went perfectly still, as if some unseen force had slammed him back against the bed.

She's your mate. I will not fuck her, but you must allow me into the meld.

Mal Ton's shuddered. The mutant light in his eyes dimmed then flared even brighter. *If your cock touches her, you die!*

With effortless ease, Mal Ton shifted his hands through the cuffs, leaving the restraints dangling from the pipe. Holy shit! She plastered herself against Fane, trembling, but Mal Ton's touch was gentle when his fingers found her thigh. He stroked her skin, working his way up to where their bodies were joined.

So beautiful, he whispered in her mind, and she released her pent-up breath. Mal Ton caressed her mound and teased her clit while Fane rolled her nipples. So many sensations. Her head began to spin and she clutched Mal Ton's sides with her knees. Tension gathered in her pussy, preparing for another release.

Move! Fane urged.

She wasn't sure if the command had been for her or Mal Ton. Dragging herself almost off Mal Ton's hardness, she paused, intending to go down slowly. He grabbed her hips with both hands and thrust to the hilt. She cried out more from surprise than the intimate impact. He braced his feet against the bed, thrusting deep with every stroke.

Fane brushed his fingers down her spine and into the crack of her ass. He'd told Mal Ton he wouldn't fuck her. So what was he…? His fingers pushed into her back passage and she cried out again. It hadn't hurt—she was still slick with lube—she just hadn't expected the forceful invasion. He matched Mal Ton thrust for thrust, stretching her even tighter.

Mal Ton grasped her hair with one hand and brought her mouth down to his. He claimed her with his tongue, using the same demanding rhythm as his cock. She was utterly filled, surrounded and overwhelmed. Fane's fingers burned, the heat reaching deep into her body. Amber sparks danced in the air, prickling her skin as they showered her back and buttocks.

Harder and hotter. She tore her mouth away from Mal Ton's, panting harshly as he pounded into her. Fear tangled with the pleasure and she clenched her teeth.

Don't resist. Surrender or we will lose him.

She took Mal Ton's face between her hands and stared into his eyes. Desperation contorted his features. She refused to look away.

He slammed into her mind. She welcomed him, saturating his fury with tenderness. He bared his teeth and bucked, rocking her against Fane's hand. She squeezed her inner muscles as tight as she could and reality exploded.

Mutant light burst through Mal Ton's skin. Sparkling waves passed over him and spilled into her. It swirled around Fane's fingers then flooded back into Mal Ton. Every pleasure synapse she possessed fired and she screamed in ecstasy. Mal Ton's shout echoed off the walls as they clung to each other.

Long moments later Fane carefully withdrew. The subtle movement launched a powerful aftershock and Lorelle sighed.

"I should twist off your hand, you son of a bitch," Mal Ton muttered. His eyes were heavy-lidded and bright teal again.

"That son of a bitch just saved your life," she objected.

Fane chucked and crawled off the end of the bed. "This just proves we were successful. Mal Ton is his charming self again."

Chapter Five

so

Raising his face to the warm downpour, Mal Ton arched his neck and savored the sting of rain against his skin. The climate domes on Stilox protected its inhabitants from the elements, provided them with an environment suitable for existence, but little else. It never rained, never snowed. The wind was recycled and simulated.

He tugged off his shirt and tossed it aside, spreading his arms as the rain pelted his torso. Lightning branched across the sky, followed instantaneously by a deafening crash of thunder. He laughed, exhilarated by the untamed energy evident all around him, grateful to be alive.

"Looks like you're feeling better?"

Mal Ton's inability to sense Fane was a testimony to Fane's power. Mal Ton spent more time filtering out other people's emotions than attempting to break through their mental shields.

"Every muscle in my body aches and I'm still not sure what happened, but Ostan assures me I'll recover." He grabbed his shirt off the ground and ducked beneath the archway where Fane stood. "Thank you."

"Your thanks should go to Lorelle not me." Fane leaned his shoulder against the side of the archway and folded his arms over his chest. Lightning forked dramatically, the sudden flash of light accenting Fane's high, hollow cheekbones.

Mal Ton had heard stories about the leader of the Mutant Underground for years. It was only when a recent crisis brought them face-to-face that Mal Ton realized he had known Fane most of his life. Their shared past was a closely guarded secret. Fane had good reason for allowing the rest of the world to believe he was dead.

"How is Lorelle?" Mal Ton asked, focusing again on the present. "She was still with Ostan when I left the clinic."

"She went to check on the others. Our newest guest has a hard time relaxing."

Unable to untangle the emotions knotting his gut, he settled for the obvious question. "Were her scans clean?"

"The virus is already in remission. By tomorrow it will be completely bound."

Mal Ton let her image fill his mind. He didn't need to close his eyes to see her in perfect detail, feel her moving over him while her gaze bore into his. The crisis was past. They'd vanquished the virus and his spontaneous shift, so why did he still hunger for her?

He released the half-formed fantasy with a sigh. "Were you able to contact Andrea?"

Fane nodded. "She insists her documentation regarding the genetic anomaly was never made public. She has no idea how Chancellor Howyn learned about their longevity."

How Howyn learned was not all that important. He knew and he obviously planned to incorporate the anomaly into his genetic arsenal. "What's our next move? The fewer people who know about the humans, the better off they'll be. Countless races would be anxious to get their hands on a group of women who don't age."

"Sean is moving them to a safe house tomorrow. As you said, we can't keep them here."

Mal Ton stiffened. There was no way in hell Lorelle was… Why should he care if she left? She meant nothing to him. Necessity brought them together for a series of intense encounters. There was nothing more to it than that.

"And after the safe house?" He tried to sound casual and failed.

"That's up to them. I'll discourage them from returning to Earth, but we have no right to keep them." After a thoughtful pause, Fane said, "Ostan is sending Lorelle's samples to Andrea."

"Why? You said the counteragent worked."

"It did, but her DNA is still…evolving."

"What the hell does that mean?" Mal Ton faced his friend and scowled. "No one mutates that quickly."

"Not ordinarily."

"Just spell it out. I'm too tired to spar with you."

"Ostan couldn't explain what's happening to her. That's why he's asking for Andrea's input."

"Has Lorelle developed new symptoms?" Some people temporarily mirrored a mutant's abilities after they'd been intimate. Mutants had to be careful who they fucked.

"She spontaneously learned Protarian. At first she could only understand it, now she is able to speak it fluently as well."

"Stranger things have happened. Is she in any danger?"

"Ostan can't be sure until her DNA stabilizes." They lapsed into silence and watched the rain. After a few moments Fane asked, "How are you going to tell her?"

"Tell her what?"

Fane chuckled. "Denying it won't make it go away. She's your mate and we both know it."

"Seconds don't have mates."

"You do," Fane argued.

The subject always made Mal Ton irritable. Stilox males with Type B sperm were considered inferior, worthy to fuck but not to be primary mates. Even his mutant abilities didn't change the fact that he was a Second.

"It makes no sense." He shook his head so violently droplets of water went flying. "She's *human*. How could she have triggered a soul bonding?"

Fane shrugged and tried to hide his smile. "All I know is what I sensed and what I saw. When the inhibitor wore off you were not feral, you were in the grip of bonding fever. Lorelle is your mate."

Even as his brain rebelled against the concept his body ached for her. "That's why you didn't fuck her."

"You had to have energy, but there was no way I was going to interfere with a soul bonding."

Mal Ton scrubbed his face with both hands, too exhausted to process the full import of what Fane was saying. "You mistook her sexual frenzy for…"

Fane slapped him on the back as he turned away. "Go see if you can continue these denials after you've touched her again."

Reluctantly donning his wet shirt, Mal Ton strode back into the hideout. Fane had to be mistaken. Soul bondings didn't happen spontaneously. The great hall was mostly deserted, the fires banked for the night.

The other humans had been given rooms on the main level of the complex. He strode down the short corridor and heard the hushed timbre of female voices. Long before he could understand their words, he recognized Lorelle's voice. The sound sent tingles down his spine and caused her image to flare to life within his mind. This couldn't be happening. The last thing he needed in his life was a reluctant mate.

* * * * *

"Where have you been?" Karla rose from her cot and gave Lorelle a firm hug. "When you didn't return last night, we didn't know what to think."

"I'm fine," Lorelle told her. "My condition was farther advanced than yours so I required…"

"I understand. We've all agreed it's better to put everything behind us. The doctor said we'll recover and that's all that matters."

"When can we go home?" one of the others asked.

Home? They still didn't understand the full scope of the crisis. None of them could ever go home again. She cleared her throat and chose her words carefully. "I'm not sure Earth is the safest place for us anymore."

"How can you say that?" Karla slipped her hands into the pockets of her simple pants. They had all been given utilitarian clothes with adjustable waists and short sleeves. The outfits looked very much like medical scrubs.

"Haven't you wondered why Andrea never told us about the genetic anomaly?" Lorelle asked.

"I'm sure you have it all figured out."

She wasn't sure why Karla sounded so hostile, but the others were waiting silently for her explanation. "Can you think of a race more fixated on youth than humans? Every government and medical institution on the planet will be scrambling to get their hands on us now."

"But they don't know about us," Karla argued.

"Yes they do. Three weeks before we were kidnapped I applied for an upgraded security clearance. A complete DNA profile was part of that process. According to the Vestaburg Alliance, governments are required to report medical findings with global ramifications to the steering committee."

Karla snorted. "As if North America has ever adhered to that condition."

"It doesn't matter," Lorelle insisted. "Even if it's just one government, our lives will never be the same."

"So we should stay here? How will these—mutants keep us safe?"

The others remained silent as Karla grew more aggressive.

"Their situation is not that different from ours. They're trying to prevent exploitation and—"

"My God, was he *that* good? One night in his bed and you're ready to join his war?" Karla's bitter jibe made the others snicker.

"This has nothing to do with Mal Ton."

"Well, unlike you, I want to be as far away from this godforsaken place as I can get. One war might be just as good as another for a professional soldier, but I have a life back on Earth. We were lured here under false pretenses. I intend to go home."

Lorelle didn't argue. She wasn't even sure the mutants had the ability to take them back to Earth, so the debate was a waste of time.

"How long will they keep us here?" Karla's mood was still prickly.

"Sean is going to take you to a safe house tomorrow," Mal Ton said from the doorway.

"And how long do we have to stay there?" Karla grumbled.

"You're no longer prisoners. We'll do everything in our power to keep you safe and provide you with options. But Lorelle is right. Returning to Earth would be dangerous."

She shot Lorelle a resentful look then changed the subject. "How did you guys learn our language so fast? Sean hardly even has an accent."

"I learned Earthish for my last mission to your homeworld. Sean has his own ways of acquiring new skills."

"You've been to Earth?" Karla latched on to that fact with obvious interest. "When? Why?"

"The Protarians were going to kidnap Andrea Raynier, so I sabotaged their mission and took her to Stilox instead."

"Were you in any way responsible for our kidnapping?"

"No. As Andrea said, the Protarians took you from Earth and Max shot down your ship before we learned what was happening."

A long pause followed and Lorelle gave in to her need to look at Mal Ton. He'd stayed near the doorway as he patiently answered Karla's questions. His tall form nearly eclipsed the threshold and his skin had an odd, moist sheen. He looked as if he'd just stepped out of a shower fully dressed.

"Lorelle, may I speak with you?" he asked.

"Didn't you two *speak* enough last night?"

Lorelle ignored the whispered taunt and moved across the room. She followed Mal Ton down the hallway and out into the massive common room. With smoldering firelight and stone floors the chamber made her feel as if she had stepped back in time.

"There was electricity in the clinic. Why is the rest of the building so primitive?"

"Anyone that peeks in through a window sees an abandoned hotel that's been taken over by refugees. It's crucial that we blend in with the rest of Old Towne."

"No one notices the spaceship?"

"Shuttles and transports aren't as uncommon as you'd think. We are in the heart of Sanctum, Protaria's capital city."

"If this is going to be a lengthy conversation, can we go outside? The last thing I want right now is to see the inside of any room."

"It's raining."

Reaching over with a soft smile, she pulled his damp shirt away from his arm. "That didn't stop you."

His form-fitting outfit left little to the imagination. Even so, her gaze gravitated toward the fastenings. He looked so much better wearing nothing at all. The doctor insisted she was free from the effects of the virus, yet one look at Mal Ton was all it took to set her senses on fire again. She wanted to peel away his clothes and let her fingers explore every centimeter of his muscular body.

He held out his hand with the hint of a smile. She placed her fingers on his and braced herself for the electric awareness she felt each time they touched. Heat sank into her flesh and her nipples gathered against the clean shirt the doctor had given her. Mal Ton's thumb brushed across her palm and made her shiver.

"Are you sure you want to go outside?"

She heard the challenge in his tone and understood the inference. If she'd rather go back to his bedroom, he was agreeable. Damn it. She'd never been this easy before.

"I need to see the sky."

They exited through the back door and hurried down an alley. Darkness had long since fallen, adding an eerie quality to the ramshackle setting. They passed boarded-up shops and vacant lots. Derelict vehicles from a variety of eras littered the street, making it obvious the area hadn't supported ground traffic in a very long time.

"Why was the chancellor after Andrea in the first place? This world is more technologically advanced than Earth. Or most of it is, anyway."

"Building ships and transcribing DNA are two very different things. The Protarians have been trying to engineer a superbeing for longer than I can remember. The chancellor likely investigated Andrea to see if she could offer a fresh perspective and found out she'd stumbled onto something far more valuable."

"Like arresting the aging process?"

"Exactly."

They entered a small park through an arch in the perimeter wall. Lorelle looked around in amazement. Indigenous plants had overtaken the flowerbeds and the footpath was all but lost in the untended grass. Trees had been planted at regular intervals. Their branches arched and entwined, creating a leafy canopy for the forgotten haven. It must have been stunning during its heyday.

"According to our information, the ship left Earth with twenty human females." Mal Ton's deep voice drew her attention away from their surroundings and back to his handsome face.

She nodded. "Most of the women agreed to participate in an offworld research project. It was supposed to last two years and they were each going to be generously compensated for their participation. It was only when the final three were dragged aboard the ship in restraints that the others realized the entire thing was a setup."

"You were one of the final three?"

"I had no desire to leave Earth, and their con was so transparent it was laughable." She picked her way along the barely visible path, too anxious to stand still. The breeze felt wonderful against her flushed face, but tension gripped her stomach as unwanted memories rolled through her mind. "I knew my government was involved when my death was staged during a top-secret mission. The Protarians couldn't have made me disappear without the help of someone on the inside."

"Everyone on Earth thinks you're dead?"

"I thought I was dead for a while." She shuddered, wending her way along a section of hedgerow so overgrown Mal Ton had to walk behind her. "We were halfway to Protaria before I regained consciousness. The others figured out Andrea was the only thing we all had in common and that's about as far as we got when the ship exploded."

As she neared the end of the hedgerow, moonlight revealed a fallen tree blocking the path. The trunk reached her hips and branches stabbed into the hedge. Her pulse leapt and her eyes narrowed. He'd known this was here! He'd stalked her so skillfully she hadn't realized she was being hunted.

Turning around, she found Mal Ton half a step away. He grinned, his teeth gleaming in the moonlight. If they made love again she'd have no justification for her brazen behavior. The realization did nothing to ease her restlessness. She wanted Mal Ton with far more than a physical ache.

"Not a very hospitable welcome to our star system." His deep voice caressed her then he moved closer, crowding her and surrounding her without actually touching.

She refused to be intimidated by his tactics. Leaning against the tree, she peered into his eyes. "How did you get drawn into this war?"

He shook his head and pivoted to the side, leaning against the tree beside her. "The way you phrased that reveals how little you know about the current situation. This war has been going on for three hundred years."

"Three hundred years?" She tried to wrap her mind around the magnitude.

"Andrea used that same derisive tone and it made me curious enough to research Earth's history. Yours is not a peaceful people. Various factions on your planet have been at war off and on for *thousands* of years."

She laid her hand on his arm, resisting the urge to stroke him. "I didn't mean to insult you. I belong to Earth's largest military. I can't criticize you for something I'm actively involved in myself. It's just surprising that there have been no periods of peace in three hundred years."

"Decades have gone by with no overt hostilities, but the issues remain. Does that mean one war ended and a new one began, or is it all one drawn-out conflict?"

"How long have you been fighting?"

"My entire life. I volunteered as a youth and never looked back."

An odd catch in his tone made her ask, "How old are you?"

He shot her a sidelong glance and smiled. "Older than I look."

"Older and stronger?" She returned his smile. "What other secrets are you hiding?"

He caught her chin lightly between his thumb and forefinger. "We have this all backward. According to Earth's customs, couples are supposed to spend time together and get to know each other before they become lovers."

"According to Earth's customs? Are things so very different here?"

"It's more the situation than the planet. Couples tend to take a more direct approach in times of crisis regardless of their location."

"Are we a couple?" She tried to avert her gaze, but he wouldn't let her. "You saved my life and I returned the favor. The score is even. We can simply walk away."

"I don't want to walk away."

Ignoring the heat rolling through her abdomen, she focused on the logical disadvantages to pursuing a relationship with this aggressive stranger. "We hardly know each other. Our time together has been shaped by outside forces. Without the virus and the danger, we might not even like each other."

"Are you still attracted to me? Because you're all I can think about. As for knowing each other, we just took the fast track. Most couples flirt and tease, revealing their true selves gradually over time. Our spirits melded. I understand you better than any human ever could. Your intelligence means more to you than your beauty. You are proud of your accomplishments, yet frustrated by your isolation. Many people consider you their friend while few actually know you as well as they think they do. And you are far more tenderhearted than you will ever admit."

She pushed his hand away from her face, not trusting herself to resist his touch. "Unfortunately I'm not empathic. I felt you in my mind. I know there's still some sort of link between us, but I don't know you any better now than I did two days ago."

That wasn't exactly true. He'd saved her life at great risk to his own and Fane's loyalty spoke volumes about Mal Ton's character. She'd stumbled upon a bona fide hero. Still, strategy was her life. Rushing in blindly wasn't only foolish, it was dangerous. She had to slow him down and do a better job of resisting their attraction. There was more at stake than her feelings.

"I don't want you to leave." The longing in his statement sent tingles down her spine.

"I'm not going anywhere. I want to help you find the other survivors."

A rare smile parted his lips and his eyes gleamed in the moonlight. "Your insight would be greatly appreciated."

He obviously thought she was using the rescue mission as an excuse, and to some degree she was. This was having little effect on their smoldering desire.

Think. Focus. Now try again.

"I know my sister survived the crash, but I have no idea where they took her." Guilt strengthened her resolve and she stepped away from the fallen log, putting some distance between them. "I won't rest until I know she's safe."

His large hand closed around her upper arm, halting her retreat. "Your sister was on the transport?"

Concern for Brianna had tormented her ever since they left Earth. "I was one of Dr. Raynier's first human trials. When the treatment worked on me, I told Andrea about Brianna. Andrea had successfully transcribed women with a variety of fertility issues and she was ready to take on a new condition. Brianna had just been diagnosed with MS."

"What is MS?" His fingers loosened, lingering against her arm in a subtle caress.

"Multiple sclerosis. It degenerates the central nervous system, gradually robbing a person of everything from sensation to mobility to sight and hearing." She still didn't turn around. Thoughts of Brianna made it impossible for Lorelle to control her expressions. "Medications can slow the progress, but many are still trapped within a malfunctioning body until they die. It's not a diagnosis anyone wants to hear. Dr. Raynier agreed to test Brianna and see if she would qualify for the program."

"Brianna's DNA was transcribed twice, like yours?"

"She was number twenty. After Brianna, no one was transcribed more than once. We had no idea the significance of that at the time, of course."

He didn't reply immediately and Lorelle crossed her arms over her chest. Brianna hadn't exhibited any symptoms before the crash, but she was one of the last to be brought onboard. Lorelle couldn't help wondering where Brianna was and how she was being treated.

"You can't blame yourself for Brianna's situation. If you hadn't gotten her into the program, she would be suffering from a terminal illness."

"Instead she's on an alien world, likely infected with a ruthlessly engineered virus that will turn her into a sex-crazed animal." She glanced over her shoulder. "I'm not sure which is worse."

He pulled her toward him and turned her around. "We'll find her and the other survivors because we won't stop trying until we do."

"I wish I could draw. I'm almost sure I saw their leader."

"You saw Max?" His fingers tightened against her upper arms. "Why didn't you say something before? Max is a phantom. He's commanding this rebellion from the shadows. Everyone knows his name, but we haven't been able to find anyone who has actually seen him."

"I didn't realize he was giving orders until I spontaneously learned Protarian. Do you have any idea how that happened by the way?"

"I have a language interface. It's possible you absorbed a cluster of my nanites and they downloaded Protarina into your brain."

"Wonderful. Can they download anything but random languages?"

"I don't think so. None of my nanites are harmful." He wrapped his fingers around the back of her neck and caressed her jaw with his thumb. "What did Max say and what does he look like? This could be really important."

"He has dark hair and glowing amber eyes." She shook her head with a sigh. "That's not much help, I know. That's why I wish I could draw."

"What did he say?" Impatience crept into his tone as Mal Ton repeated the question.

"Two crewmembers survived the crash. Max arrived a short time later. He told the first to take three of us to 'pirautiel'. Does that mean anything to you?" Mal Ton shook his head, so she went on. "Matthew was the other surviving crewmember. He's the one you morphed into. Max told him to take four of us to sector nine. I'm presuming that's where you found us. The last location made no more sense than the first. It sounded like 'my stressaphy'."

"To which location did they take your sister?"

"I don't know. It was dark and she was led away by one of the men who arrived with Max." Mal Ton took her hand and started back along the hedgerow. "Where are we going?"

"To see if Fane can make sense out of any of this."

Aubrey Ross

Chapter Six

☙

"I knew you could read my mind." Lorelle's gentle smile made Mal Ton ball his fists. She was flirting with Fane.

"I never told you I couldn't." Fane must have sensed a blast of jealousy. He looked at Mal Ton as he smiled. "I only told you the image you transmitted to me didn't require the ability. Why don't you tell Mal Ton what you were imagining?"

Lorelle gasped and slapped Fane on the arm. Mal Ton scowled. He didn't want them touching each other. He hated their comfortable camaraderie. Fane knew they were mates even if Lorelle had yet to accept it.

Fane turned back to Lorelle, his expression guarded again. "Focus on the leader. Remember every detail about his appearance, the tone of his voice, how he moved."

Lorelle closed her eyes and Fane pressed in close behind her like he had been when he cupped her breasts and—

Enough, Mal Ton. You're distracting me.

I know you were cautious once I was aware, but how far did it go before the inhibitor wore off?

Fane's hands dropped to her shoulders and he gave her a little squeeze. "Your lover is disrupting my concentration. Will you please tell him what happened before he regained consciousness?"

Lorelle opened her eyes and raised her chin. "First of all Mal Ton doesn't own me. If I had fucked you, it's none of his business—not to mention it would have been done to save his ungrateful hide. Second, he might not trust me, but he has no reason to mistrust you. I'm not going to dignify his attitude

98

with a response." She guided Fane's hands to her head and said, "Carry on."

You haven't told her?

Annoyed by the amusement in Fane's tone, Mal Ton pulled out one of the desk chairs and sat. He would tell her once she'd recovered from all the other surprises. Lorelle wouldn't consider leaving until her sister was found, so the mate issue could wait a little longer.

"I can barely see him," Fane said. "Can you make the image any clearer?"

After a short pause, she shook her head. "That's what he looked like to me. Dark hair, shadowy features and glowing eyes."

Fane lowered his hands. "Neither of the locations you mentioned means anything to me. Either they're some sort of code or you're not remembering exactly what he said. His language didn't mean anything to you then, so it wouldn't be surprising if your mind twisted the word or phrase."

"How do we untwist them?" Mal Ton asked. "This is all we have to work with right now."

"Take her to the data center and have one of the technicians run the words through the Protarian database."

Mal Ton stiffened at the suggestion. Renée was the best stream analyst they had and she'd been panting after him since he arrived. Was Fane amusing himself?

"I told her to back off." A hint of a smile tugged at one corner of Fane's mouth. "Do you want me to reinforce the command?"

"I can handle Renée." He stood and motioned Lorelle toward the door to Fane's office.

"Who is Renée?" Lorelle waited until they were alone in the corridor to pose the question.

"One of Fane's people. She's…interested in me."

"I'm pretty sure we met. Shoulder-length brown hair and big brown eyes?"

"That could be a lot of people, but the description fits Renée."

They turned to the right and followed the sloping passageway to a door that accessed the abandoned subway tunnels. The air was stale and the ground cluttered, sections of the tunnel nearly blocked by collapse. He ignited the mutant intensity of his gaze and cringed. The additional illumination was a mixed blessing. Walking was easier, but now they could see the rat-infested debris.

She's a soldier, you ass. Surely she's seen worse than this.

Undeterred by their dismal surroundings, she walked along at his side. "You don't return her interest?"

"Not in the least." Her persistence pleased him. If her feelings for him had abated with the virus, Renée's interest wouldn't bother her. "Renée is a mutant groupie. Her own abilities are minimal, so she augments them as often as she can."

"And how does she do that?" She ignored his proffered hand as they climbed over a massive pile of rubble.

Stubborn and independent to the end. Her antics made him smile. "Some people absorb our abilities if we have sex with them more than once. The abilities are always temporary, but it's dangerous for several reasons."

"A spy could figure out who can do what if they are willing to have sex indiscriminately."

"They could, and do."

"If you know Renée is doing this, can't she be…exiled or something?"

"Renée isn't a spy. She just envies those with more unusual abilities."

"Like you and Fane?"

"Yes." He climbed onto a grimy platform that had once been a subway station and helped her out of the culvert dissecting the two sides. "We're almost there."

She followed him in thoughtful silence as they climbed briefly to street level. "Why was this section of the city deserted?"

"Resources. As the population diminished, it made sense to consolidate."

They were on the fringes of Old Towne now. The lights and sounds of Sanctum were just out of reach. Her gaze lingered on the huge metropolis as he led her into an alley between two tall buildings. He pulled open a nondescript door and ushered her inside.

The data center was located in the basement of a derelict office building, somewhat isolated from the rest of the Underground. Twelve workstations, each with multiple screens and a sound booth from which the mutants could monitor Protarian communications had been assembled in one corner of the cavernous room.

"This is unexpected," Lorelle said softly. "Where do they get power for all this equipment?"

"We tap into their primary grid," the young man nearest them told her. "We're like tiny insects. We take a nibble here and a nibble there, continually modulating the entry points so they don't realize they're infested."

Their conversation drew the attention of several technicians. Renée pushed back from her workstation and hurried toward them.

"Mal Ton!" Her smile was radiant until she noticed Lorelle. "What can I do for you?"

"Info search. We have a couple possible locations, but the words might be distorted."

"No problem. I can compile a list of similar matches and prioritize them with specific criteria. Are you still trying to locate the humans Max intercepted?"

"Yes."

Renée walked back to her workstation. After a quick, assessing glance, she ignored Lorelle completely. Mal Ton took Lorelle by the hand and followed Renée.

"All right. What am I searching for?"

"The first one is pirautiel or pirateal," Lorelle supplied.

"I'll input both and see which generates more possibilities."

"The locations will have to be isolated or provide an environment where incarceration is the norm," Mal Ton explained.

"Are you certain they're still on Protaria? Captives would be a whole lot easier to hide on Stilox. That entire planet is a wasteland."

"As long as you don't need to breathe," he reminded.

"True. Locations within the climate domes might be a bit harder to find."

"See what you can come up with on Protaria. If nothing fits, we'll broaden our search."

"Fair enough." Renée continued constructing the search criteria. "You said the first one is pirautiel. Do you need another search?"

Lorelle nodded. "The second phrase was 'my stressaphy'."

"Or something similar?"

"I'm afraid so," Mal Ton said.

"You know, Max might have been referring to a person," Lorelle mused. "'Take them to Fane' as opposed to 'take them to the Underground'."

"If I'm searching for people too, this might take awhile."

"Send a runner as soon as you have anything useful."

* * * * *

Lorelle woke suddenly as awareness jarred her senses. Mal Ton lay behind her with one of his arms draped over her waist. His scent surrounded her, enticing and arousing her. She enjoyed the intimacy for a moment as sleep's haze receded from her mind. Why were they in bed again? He'd agreed to give her some space and let her sort through her feelings without his undeniably distracting presence. Hadn't he?

They'd returned to the main hideout and scrounged together a quick meal. She'd hardly been able to keep her eyes open, so Mal Ton insisted she get some sleep. A brief argument had followed when she'd refused to return to his bedroom. Finally he'd relented and escorted her to a guest room.

She rolled onto her back and shook his shoulder. "Mal Ton, wake up." Candles sputtered to life an instant before his eyes opened. He moved his knee between her legs and shifted his hand to her breast. She shoved with more force, anger flaring through her confusion. "What the hell are you doing here?"

He looked around, blinking in the candle's wavering light. "Why are we in a guestroom?"

"No, why are *you* in *my* room? You promised to back off."

With obvious reluctance he disentangled their bodies and sat. "I must have...sleepwalked."

"Yeah right." She scooted off the side of the bed and grabbed her discarded pants. "You walked down the hall and hacked the door lock while you were sound asleep?"

He glanced at the door then back at the bed, his confounded expression almost believable. "I was too restless to sleep, so I read through some files Fane gave me. I must have dozed off at my desk. Our bond is stronger than I realized. I honestly don't remember coming in here."

She heaved an exaggerated sigh. "Lust isn't a bond, it's an inconvenience. We are not going to fuck again. Just get over it!"

He launched himself across the bed and dragged her beneath him in one lightning-fast motion. Snatching the pants out of her hand, he tossed them back on the floor. "It would be easier to believe your argument if the scent of your arousal weren't making me dizzy. I can't explain it. This doesn't generally happen to Seconds. All I know is this is real. You are my mate and I am yours. Denials are a waste of time."

His mouth covered hers with the same possessive aggression that defined their every embrace. He pressed her into the mattress, urging her legs apart with his knees. Capturing her wrists, he drew her hands over her head and rubbed his erection against the apex of her thighs.

She gasped and his tongue thrust into her mouth. This was different than the virus, yet undeniably sexual. Her panties and his clothes were no barrier for the heat radiating off his body. He moved against not inside her, but the simulation was no less exciting. Her inner muscles throbbed and her clit tingled. She could hardly breathe.

"Has lust ever felt like this? Has your body ever demanded its Master?"

Jerking against his hold, she turned her head to the side. "No one is my Master!"

The jerk just laughed. "We'll start with mate and work toward Master. Do you deny wanting me?"

"It's called lust, asshole," she snapped. "I already admitted that I want you."

His gaze narrowed and he shifted both her wrists into one hand, freeing his other to touch her. "I didn't ask for this. The female triggers the soul bonding. *You* did this to *me*."

"Well, I sure as hell didn't do it intentionally." A bit of the fight went out of her as each frantic breath filled her head with his scent. She longed to feel him deep inside her, ached with every fiber of her being. "How do we turn it off?"

"We don't."

He found her nipple through her top and teased the sensitive crest. She wiggled and tossed her head. This couldn't be happening. She didn't want an alien lover, much less a mate. Brianna was still out there. Lorelle didn't have time for erotic games! His hand slipped beneath her top and enjoyed the hard peaks he'd created. Her body had no problem with surrender, but her mind rebelled.

"I can feel the heat of your pussy," he pressed closer. "Are you as wet as I suspect?"

Keeping her legs wedged open with his torso, he lifted his body off hers and settled on his knees. He eased his hand inside her panties and traced her slit with his fingertips. His gaze bore into hers and reality narrowed as if by his decree. This was Mal Ton, her mate, her…Master.

Her heart thundered and her body burned. A tangible current arced between them, resonating through her entire body. She stared into his eyes and felt her heart take on the driving rhythm of his pulse.

"Is this lust?" His finger circled her opening, accenting the ache and how wet she'd become. "The virus is in remission and my crisis is long past. Why do we need each other so badly?"

"I'll never be your slave." Even as she whispered the vow, her hips arched, driving his finger into her core.

"Never?" He pulled back, robbing her of the tiny hint of fullness.

"Stop teasing me! Yes, I want your cock, so what? Why do you have to make it into a mystical bond?"

"It is a mystical bond. It's elemental and undeniable and wonderful." With an impatient snarl, he ripped the sides of her panties and dragged the fabric out from underneath her. His aggression drove her arousal higher, increasing the tension and the heat. He added a second finger and shuttled in and out of her creamy passage. She rocked into each shallow thrust, wanting so much more than his fingers. "You need to stop lying to yourself."

She bit back her argument. As long as he kept touching her, she didn't care what he said. His thumb brushed across her clit and her pussy clenched. Yes! Just a few more... He dragged his fingers out and she went wild.

Kicking and bucking, she jerked her hand free and lashed out at him. He caught her wrist an instant before her nails slashed his face. His chest pressed against her until her struggle was reduced to furious yanks and muttered curses.

"During the second phase of bonding fever the female becomes combative. The male must overpower her, compel her to submit, proving his strength and virility." He whispered the words into her ear as he rubbed his shaft against her mound. "Can you explain the emotions seething within you? You want to kill me, but you want to fuck me even more. Sound about right?"

"You're deranged. I'm just pissed off."

"Really?" He released her and rocked back on his heels, challenge gleaming in his eyes.

As if someone else were controlling her body, she reared up and jerked his vest down along his arms, desperate for the feel of his naked flesh. Her mouth fastened on to one of his nipples while her hands stroked and squeezed. God, he felt amazing, hot, hard and...

Her ravenous gaze fixed on his crotch and she reached for the fastenings at the top of his pants. He caught her wrists, halting her determined quest.

"Each time we do this the bond grows stronger until it's permanent. Do you understand that?"

She shoved against his chest and collapsed across the bed. "If you're not going to fuck me, then get out. I can't wait any longer." Why did her voice sound so shrill? She stared at the long, thick ridge in his pants and skimmed her hands up and down her body. "I've done just fine by myself for years."

Unable to stop herself from provoking him, she parted her folds with one hand and rubbed her clit with the other. This wasn't her. She would never behave so brazenly.

He growled and pounced, diving beneath her legs and grabbing her wrists in a skillful maneuver that left her utterly helpless. Her legs draped over his shoulders and his hands felt like iron manacles. His tongue thrust deep into her cunt, accepting her brash offer. She wiggled, rubbing her folds against his mouth, demanding his tongue on her clit.

She came in shocking bursts of sensation that made her arch and moan. He lapped at her cream then sucked her essence directly from her core. It wasn't enough! She needed to be stretched and filled, overwhelmed and — claimed.

Knowing it was irrational yet unable to resist the impulse, she began fighting against him again. She twisted and tugged, wrestling one leg down between them. He simply followed her for a while, savoring the proof of her release as she struggled to escape his hold.

She didn't want him to let go, so why the hell was she fighting him? Fear surged through the lust, followed immediately by confusion. She sagged onto the bed. "What's happening to me?"

He raised his head and looked into her eyes. His gaze was warm and surprisingly tender, though a ring of mutant light glittered around the teal. "We're feeding one of those mystical bonds you don't believe exist."

His lips covered hers and his tongue filled her mouth with the proof of her surrender. She was his already. She'd sensed it the first time they touched. Ignoring her chaotic thoughts, she returned his kiss. He wasn't even holding her anymore. She clung to him while he struggled out of his pants. He paused to tug her shirt off over her head then positioned himself between her legs.

She shook, her senses stretched to the brink of insanity. He guided his cock toward her entrance and she twisted away. To her horror, he laughed, enjoying the challenge. He flipped her over and moved her thighs apart with his knees. Before she could crawl forward, he wrapped his arm around her hips and drove his full length into her pussy.

Her body welcomed his with rhythmic pulses and slick cream. He controlled her with the weight of his body and the inescapable penetration of his cock. Slowly, ever-so slowly he pulled back then thrust into her again. She trembled beneath him, savoring the fullness and the heat. He grasped her hips and began a slow, deep rhythm that detonated new sensations and made her moan. She clawed the bedding and arched her back, taking all he had to give.

She slapped back at him, knowing he'd grab her arms and complete the domination. His cock filled her, each individual thrust a separate claim on her body and her mind. She surrendered to his aggression, secure within the shelter of his strength.

His being pushed into her mind, the telepathic joining every bit as demanding as the motion of his hips.

Mine! Say it. You are mine.

I am yours and you are mine. She tightened her inner muscles and blasted him with raw, possessive passion. If she was going to lose herself in this madness, she wasn't going over alone.

Yes, come for me. Scream my name as you come.

Scalding spasms of pleasure burst within her. She cried out and buried her face in the bedding. He thrust deep and released his seed, a hoarse cry escaping from his throat. The ripples went on and on. He shuddered, his abdomen flexing against her back. Then he nipped her firmly on the shoulder.

She yelped and shivered, a powerful aftershock making her moan. "What was that for?"

"We're going to have to do it all again."

"Not that I'm complaining, but did we do something wrong?"

"You didn't say my name. The bonding isn't official until you scream my name."

Glancing over her shoulder, she saw mischief shimmering in his eyes.

Chapter Seven

≈

Mal Ton pressed Lorelle against his chest and indulged in a contented smile. Warm water flowed over their naked bodies, easing sore muscles and helping them relax. Images of their first night together teased his memory and threatened to abolish their peaceful lethargy.

He'd never imagined life with a mate. Before last night there had been no reason. Genetics and nano-enhancements determined his course. He was a soldier, a shifter and a Second. Any one of the three turned most women away, so how had—

"What's a Second?" Lorelle eased back and met his gaze as steam swirling around her lovely face.

The question startled him. Was she already attuned to his feelings or had her musings simply been similar to his? Their expanding bond made it difficult for him to distinguish her feelings from his. He was accustomed to filtering people out. The inability to isolate himself from her felt odd yet comfortable.

"Why do you ask?" He didn't want to get into Stilox physiology right now. It felt wonderful just to hold her.

"You were surprised that I had triggered this bond because I'm human and you're a Second. What makes you a Second?"

"It will be a long, boring conversation. Can't you think of a more enjoyable way to spend our time?"

She wiggled away from his wandering hands. "We spent most of the night *enjoying* each other. I need to understand what's happening to me, what's happening to us."

With a frustrated sigh, he turned off the water and pushed open the shower door. "Let's find something to eat and I'll answer your questions."

"Thank you."

They dressed and descended to the ramshackle kitchen. The remnants of the morning meal had been tucked away in one of the ancient ovens. An insulated container ensured the food remained hot.

"The kitchen has no power source." She lowered her voice to a conspirator's whisper as she voiced her observation. "How was the food prepared?"

"Fane's people either replicated it on one of the lower levels or 'borrowed' it from a restaurant in Sanctum. Sean isn't the only one who can move about undetected." Mal Ton carried the thurmohamper to the tiny table in the far corner of the spacious room. The dining room was in better shape, but the chances of being overheard were greater. He waited until they were seated and had begun eating before he spoke again. "How familiar are you with human physiology?"

"I'm a soldier, not a scientist." She raised her cup of steaming cirgra tea. "This is nice."

"It's the only Stilox beverage Andrea will drink without protest. I suspected you and your friends might like it."

"Good call." She took another sip. "Sorry for the distraction. I'm listening."

It was hard to concentrate when everything she did fascinated him. Her hands were strong, the nails blunted, yet her long, tapered fingers were undeniably feminine. Much like her touch, her hands… He shook away the irrelevant tangent and focused on the information she'd requested.

"The people of Stilox have evolved into a triploid species."

"I have no idea what that means."

"Our DNA has three strands instead of two."

"What are the advantages of having a third strand? And what does it have to do with this 'Second' business?"

He rubbed his eyes with his fingertips. Perhaps he should have risked a trip to Stilox. Andrea could have explained this so much better. "I should probably take you to Ostan. I'm not a scientist either."

"I don't want to talk to the doctor about what's happening to us."

"He already knows."

"That doesn't mean I want to talk to him about it. Give it your best shot and if I still don't understand, you can take me to Ostan."

Opening his eyes, Mal Ton called upon every molecule of patience he possessed as he encapsulated the information. "Our third DNA strand makes us strong and resistant to disease. The Protarian's lentavirus would have obliterated a less-resilient species."

"I'm following you so far."

"Rather like humans have blood types, Stilox males have different types of sperm." She folded her arms on the tabletop and stared into his eyes. He obviously had her undivided attention. "There are two classifications. We simply call them A and B. Within each classification, there are numerous variations, but it requires sperm from both classifications for a female to conceive."

"Any female or just Stilox females?"

"As I understand it, the Stilox genome isn't complete in either of the two classifications. It takes a combination of A and B to produce Stilox offspring."

Her brow furrowed and she pushed the food container aside. "Did that answer my question?"

"Interspecies mating is always tricky. Protarian females are descended from the same original gene pool as Stilox, so it's not surprising that we are compatible with them. However there have been documented cases of offspring produced with five additional species."

"And in every case it took two Stilox males to produce the offspring?"

"Yes." He gave her a moment to absorb the facts. "Males with Type A sperm are considered better mates. They tend to be more caring, more patient and tolerant. Type B males are quick to anger and aggressive."

She chuckled. "I don't have to guess which type you are."

"Long ago the ratio of men to women allowed each female to have a primary and secondary mate. Because of our basic personalities more Type B males became soldiers when the war began."

"Now there are more Type A men than Type B?"

"By far. Seconds, as we're called now, typically have more than one mate. Our purpose is to protect our females when their primary mate is not available and to provide the needed…biological contribution when the couple is ready to have a child."

"That seems so callous. These couples are using you when it's necessary and ignoring you when—"

"This isn't Earth, Lorelle. Our cultures have been shaped by forces you're just beginning to understand. And I don't just mean the war. Seconds have always played a more peripheral role in our social structure."

"Doesn't our bond make you my primary mate?"

"Yes, and to my knowledge no female has ever triggered bonding fever in a Second before."

Wrapping both hands around her mug, she gazed into her cirgra tea as she asked, "How does it usually happen?"

"Seconds are predatory, aggressive and argumentative. So we leave the courting to Type A men."

"Some women like aggressive men." She glanced into his eyes before hiding her expression with her cup.

"Women enjoy fucking aggressive men, but in the long run Type A men are better able to make them happy."

"My happiness isn't dependent on anyone but me. Besides, I can be aggressive and argumentative too."

"I noticed." He chuckled. "We aren't talking about us. We're talking about the social norm."

"Sorry." The sparkle in her eyes was anything but apologetic. "Go on."

"I might have given you the wrong impression with my description. Type A men aren't spineless or malleable. Fane is a good example of a Type A male."

"But he's a soldier."

"The war has been raging for generations. We all serve the resistance in one way or another."

"We're way off course again. Please go back to the usual mating pattern for Stilox couples."

He inclined his head. "As with so many things, our courting practices have been streamlined and condensed. The Type A male tells the female he's interested in her. They exchange DNA profiles, and if each is acceptable to the other, they spend time together."

"How romantic." She shook her head and set down her cup.

"Our planet was ravaged by a biological weapon. Fallout from the catastrophe is still being discovered. It's a reasonable precaution."

"Let's say their DNA profiles are acceptable and they go out on a few dates. What happens after that?"

"The custom you're referring to doesn't exist on Stilox. When we're interested in a female, we're looking for a potential mate, not a casual amusement."

"Meaning?"

"There has to be an immediate connection or the courtship is pointless. A Stilox 'date' consists of a meal, a time of conversation and progressively more intimate exchanges. If the female's body releases pheromones while the couple kisses, they continue. If they feel no significant rise in the level of their desire, they go their separate ways."

"Does the female have control over her pheromones?"

"To some extent. The initial release is intentional, but a combination of factors determines the potency of the pheromones. If a female likes the way the male looks but is put off by his personality, she can pretend there was no chemical reaction. However once the process begins, genetic compatibility has more to do with success than physical attraction."

"The female chooses whether or not to release the pheromones, but she can't control how well they work?"

"Exactly. The pheromones spike sexual desire in both the male and female, which in turn makes the next rush of pheromones all the more potent. If the couple isn't genetically suited, the pheromones won't incite their lust no matter how pleasing they find each other."

"Are they able to function sexually without the pheromones?"

"Of course. We're talking about mating, not fucking. The physical act might be more or less the same, but there is a significant difference."

"Then we are…"

"Extremely compatible."

"Still, if we ever want to have a child, we'll have to find a Type A…helper."

Her phrasing made him laugh. "Are children a priority with you?"

"Not right now. I haven't even decided if I'm willing to put up with you on a regular basis." She smiled, assuring him she was kidding—more or less. "But if I don't smother you in your sleep, eventually I'll want children. Have you forgotten why Andrea Raynier transcribed my DNA?"

"I haven't forgotten." Andrea's process had still been experimental when Lorelle agreed to participate. Having children must be very important to her.

"You said you're older than you look. Do you have children?"

"I *had* children and grandchildren. I've outlived them all."

Unable to resist her need to touch him, Lorelle reached across the table and squeezed his hand. "I'm so sorry. I can't even imagine how horrible that must have been."

He caressed the top of her hand with his thumb, his gaze warm upon her face. "I've had many years to adjust to the loss."

"Are any of…the mothers still alive?"

"It's complicated." He eased his hand out of her light grasp and pushed back from the table. "Before the war began, an average lifespan for both Stilox and Protarians was about five hundred years. The war itself cut that in half and the biological weapons decreased it even further."

She wasn't sure what the statistics had to do with the mothers of his children, so she just nodded.

"I was recruited for an experimental program not long after the war began. The Protarians kept building more destructive weapons, so we had no choice but to build tougher soldiers. At least that's what we were told."

"How did they make you tougher?"

"We were injected with a series of nanites."

"This is what you meant when you speculated about my language skills."

"Yes. The nanites made us stronger, faster and healthier. They also allowed us to learn more rapidly and retain information indefinitely. We became extremely resistant to disease and were able to heal almost any injury."

"So you survived while others died?"

He glanced away with a stiff nod. "I never realized how unpleasant longevity would become. Everyone I cared about died and still I lived on, healthy and basically unchanged. It was as if time flowed around me."

"I can't pretend to understand all you've lived through, but I'm starting to understand what it feels like not to age."

"I suppose you are." He crossed his arms over his chest and released a long, slow sigh. "It's interesting that the woman fate chose to be my mate is struggling with a similar affliction."

How could he accept that they were mates without a second thought? Their physical attraction was undeniable, but it took more than biological compatibility to spend a lifetime with one person.

Rather than starting another argument, she said, "I don't consider an extended lifespan an affliction. But then time hasn't been flowing around me nearly as long as it has you."

After a thoughtful pause, he said, "Andrea is analyzing your DNA. Hopefully she'll be able to shed some light on what's happening to us."

"I thought you had it all figured out. We're mates, destined from conception to find each other."

He chuckled at her sarcasm. "There is no mistaking the nature of our bond. Still, it would be nice to understand the mechanism fate used to set these events in motion."

"And if Andrea can't explain it?"

"Then I'll accept that it was just meant to be." He punctuated the sentence with a casual shrug.

It would take a lot more than that for Lorelle to accept all the changes, but she was tired of fighting with herself. She wanted Mal Ton, felt safe and comfortable with him. Why not enjoy the attraction for a while and see what developed?

"Andrea was with someone when she made that recording." Lorelle stood as well and they put their dishes back into the hamper. "Do you know who it was?"

"His name is Roark Talbot. He's a scientist. They've been working together since she arrived on Stilox."

Lorelle smiled. "He called her kitten. I suspect they've been doing more than working."

"Indeed they have." He took the hamper and led her back to the kitchen. "Are you and Andrea close?"

"Not especially. She's more of an acquaintance than a friend."

"I've known Roark for years. His affection is genuine. He'll treat her well." He put the hamper in the sink and made a bland gesture toward the lower level. "I need to speak with Fane for a few minutes. Can you make it back to your bedroom alone or would you like me to—"

"I'll be fine." She was a professional soldier. She should be insulted by his concern. So why did she find the protectiveness endearing? And why was she agreeing to wait in her bedroom like a child? This world was making her soft. Soft and hot and wet...

Lorelle felt eyes following her as she crossed the great hall. But each time she glanced at the people loitering in the massive room, they looked away. The mutants were secretive and suspicious. Fane might trust her to some extent, but she was far from winning the acceptance of his people.

The stairs creaked beneath her feet and moonlight illuminated the narrow hallway. She ignored the shivers speeding down her spine and rushed toward the doorway halfway down the corridor.

It was frustrating to be so out of sorts. If she were on Earth, she would know what to do, who to question and where to search for her sister. As it was, she felt useless and helpless.

She pushed the door to her bedroom inward and automatically checked the shadowed corners before entering the room. Kicking the door shut with the heel of her boot, she took two steps toward the dresser, meaning to light a candle, when someone grabbed her from behind.

The hands were cool against the sides of her head and a presence pushed into her mind. Reacting instinctively, she widened her stance and bent her knees. She slammed her elbow backward, connecting with ribs. A soft grunt was her only reward until the hands slipped away from her head.

Pivoting on the ball of one foot, Lorelle grabbed the assailant's arm and shoved her shoulder into a lean midsection. She lifted with her legs, flinging the person up and over. The assailant landed with a louder grunt and Lorelle straddled their chest, her fingers grasping their windpipe, ready to squeeze.

"Who the hell are you and why are you in my bedroom?"

"I won't hurt you." The woman didn't sound frightened or even surprised. Some sort of twisting headdress concealed most of her face. Only her glowing amber eyes were visible in the darkness.

"I know you won't hurt me." Lorelle tightened her fingers for a second then relaxed her grip. "Answer the questions."

Mutant fire brightened, expanding until the glow surrounded Lorelle. "Don't threaten me."

With no further warning, Lorelle was flung backward. She slammed against the wall and slid to the floor, astonished yet unharmed.

The woman struggled to her feet and candles flickered to life around the room. "I was going to show you the images and leave. I saw no reason for a lengthy conversation." Candlelight revealed puckered, drooping flesh around her mismatched eyes.

Lorelle met her gaze directly, trying to conceal her apprehension. "What images? Why show them to me?"

"I thought you wanted to find the others. If I was wrong, forgive the intrusion." She turned toward the door.

"Wait!" Lorelle tried to approach but some unseen power anchored her in place. "I'm sorry I attacked you. You surprised me." The pressure eased and Lorelle was able to stand.

"I know I make people uncomfortable. I was trying to spare you the—"

"Sarah, what are you doing up here?" Mal Ton asked from the doorway.

"If you want access to my visions, you have to put up with my face." Bitterness snapped through her tone and she adjusted the fall of her veil to more completely cover her deformity.

"We have all been changed by this war." He stepped into the room and closed the door. "Some of us are able to conceal the changes and some of us are not. That doesn't alter the fact that we're all mutants. What brought you to Lorelle's room?"

Mal Ton's easy manner soothed Lorelle. Still, she wasn't ready to relax entirely.

"I had another vision. This one was harder to understand than the one that lead you to her."

"You're the one who led to my rescue?" Though Sarah didn't bother to look at her, Lorelle felt obligated to add, "Thank you."

"What did you see?" Mal Ton asked.

"The images were disturbing. I'm not honestly sure they pertain."

"It's better to be certain." With infinite care, he placed his hand on Sarah's shoulder. "Would you please share them with me?"

Lorelle was amazed by his patience. He spoke in a soft, non-confrontational tone and his expression was caring without being condescending. She'd seen flashes of his softer side before, but nothing like this.

"I don't want to do this twice. It makes more sense to show her."

Mal Ton dragged the chair away from the antique writing desk. "Have a seat, Lorelle." He was positioning her with her back to Sarah.

She won't hurt you, love. You have my word on that.

Accepting the telepathic assurance with a quick nod, Lorelle sat in the chair. Sarah pressed her hands to either side of Lorelle's head and Lorelle closed her eyes. Sarah pushed into her mind, strong yet clumsy.

Mal Ton passed energy across their link, allowing Lorelle to stabilize the transfer. The images formed in sporadic flashes of light and color. She opened her mind, accepting yet controlling the information.

A blonde woman sprawled on a rectangular pad, her legs spread, knees bent. She stroked her breasts with one hand and fucked herself with an alloy dildo. Lorelle recoiled from the image and the desperation surging through the scene. The situation was all too familiar. She already knew what the captives were enduring. How would this help her locate them?

Across the small room, a slender brunette lay naked on a similar matt. She was curled up on her side, arms wrapped around her knees. Her face was turned away, but Lorelle's pulse thundered through her veins. Brianna's hair was the same gold-tinted brown. The body type was hard to judge with her curled in on herself. Still, tension gathered with nauseating intensity.

The brunette remained in focus as colorful leaves drifted across the scene. Yellow, red and gold gradually collected until the other image was completely concealed.

The transfer faded and Sarah's hands slid to Lorelle's shoulders. "I don't understand the significance of the leaves, but they're definitely part of the vision."

Before Lorelle could reply, Sarah slipped from the room.

"What did she show you?" Mal Ton moved into her line of sight. His tone was cautious, expression guarded.

"A blonde and a brunette in the throes of…whatever you want to call what the virus does to us."

"Were either of them Brianna?"

"I'm not sure. The brunette's hair was the right color, but I couldn't see her face."

"Sarah said something about leaves. What did she mean?"

"The vision ended with autumn leaves floating down across the other images. Are there woods nearby? The trees in the park still had green leaves. When will the seasons change in this part of Protaria?"

"Summer is just winding down. We won't see autumn leaves for several weeks yet."

"Unless they took her to another part of the world."

"Before we expand the search to all of Protaria, let's see if Renée has any clues that might pull this all together."

Lorelle wasn't anxious to watch Renée devour Mal Ton with her eyes again, but he was right. They didn't have the personnel or the time to search the entire world. She tried to maintain her side of the conversation as they made their way back to the data center.

"Are there many like Sarah?" What little she'd been able to see of Sarah's face lingered in Lorelle's mind. "She must be so lonely."

"Are you referring to her appearance or her extraordinary abilities?"

"Both, I guess. If you walk down the street, no one would guess what you're capable of doing. Are more of the mutants like you or like Sarah?" They reached the subway tunnels and Mal Ton lit their way with the intensity of his gaze.

"There is no specific pattern, but those who recover quickly from the onset illness are less likely to develop mutations. When people realized this, they started prolonging their exposure to the virus in the hopes that they would trigger a useful ability."

"Are you saying Sarah did that to herself?" Disgust eroded Lorelle's pity.

"She was mildly clairvoyant before she was exposed to the virus, so chances were better that she'd mutate. Most of the ones who refused the counteragent as long as she did turned feral. She's damn lucky to be alive."

"I can't imagine trying to force my body to mutate."

He smiled and dimmed his gaze so he could look at her. "Some would argue that recoding your DNA is basically the same thing."

"I suppose. We're all playing God to some degree."

"Sean is her brother." They continued down the deserted tunnel. "Do you remember Sean?"

"The living shadow who helped you rescue me?"

"We call them specters. Their abilities are extremely rare. Sarah watched her brother's transformation and hoped she would achieve a similar result."

"And instead she doomed herself to a life in the shadows."

"The Protarians have every advantage. Sarah's sacrifice has benefited our cause more than you know."

They were silent for a time. Lorelle reevaluated her attitude. Sarah hadn't been hoping for fortune and fame. She'd selflessly risked her life to benefit the grater good.

Renée sauntered across the data center as they entered a short time later. After launching a resentful glower at Lorelle, she turned her admiring gaze on Mal Ton. "I was about to come find you." She slipped her arm around his and slowly licked her lips.

He unwound her arm before he spoke. "What were you able to learn?"

"I prioritized the locations according to probability."

"Could any of the locations be associated with autumn leaves?"

Her eyes widened and she glanced at Lorelle. "Why do you ask?"

"Sarah had another vision."

"Why did you bother me if you had Sarah working on the case?" She folded her arms across her chest and pressed her lips into a petulant frown.

"Her vision was inconclusive. Hopefully what you learned can verify what we suspect and pinpoint a location."

"Mistress Effie Merautta owns a chain of sexual training centers. Each 'den' is named after a season and indicates the various stages of a relationship." Renée rattled off the information with feigned indifference while her gaze traveled the length of Mal Ton's tall form.

"Given the images in Sarah's vision," he said thoughtfully, "it would seem we need the location of Mistress Effie's Autumn Den."

Chapter Eight

 જી

Keller leaned his elbows on his desktop and watched Cassie move about her lab. Tapping into security surveillance had been simple for someone with his clearance level. If anyone noticed the unauthorized access, he would claim he was following up on an anonymous threat. No one could blame him for verifying the well-being of the chancellor's daughter.

Her grace was mesmerizing, her beauty undeniable. Her conservative clothes couldn't hide her lush figure and her severe hairstyle only accented her features' allure. He imagined those long-fingered hands unfastening his pants and freeing his aching cock. She'd slip to her knees in front of him and part those soft pink lips as she sucked him into her mouth.

Lust pounded through his blood and fired his imagination. He'd pictured her naked on every horizontal surface in his office and in her lab. He'd imagined fucking her against the wall and on the floor. His fantasies had featured her so often he was running out of positions and variations. He rubbed his erection through his pants, not caring if a random surveillance check caught him touching himself. They couldn't see what was on his vidscreen, so let them laugh!

An interrupt signal chimed and Keller reached for his com console. The signal sounded again and he realized it was coming from Cassie's laboratory. She turned from her workstation and checked the security screen. After releasing the lock, she stood back and waited for her visitor to enter.

Her father strolled into the lab and kissed her cheeks. "You were supposed to check in this morning. I was worried about you."

"You could have commed me. I always answer for you."

Keller narrowed his gaze on the screen. Countless times he'd been forwarded right to her message center. She obviously offered him no similar pledge. Resentment battled with desire. He hated her. He wanted her. He hated himself for wanting her so badly.

"Has there been any progress?" the chancellor asked.

"The newest adjustments increased the success rate from seventy-one to eighty-three percent. As soon as I get three consecutive simulations in the nineties I'll ask for volunteers."

"I told you I have volunteers lined up already. Won't actual testing be more accurate than simulations?"

"And I told you I'm not willing to risk volunteer testing until the simulations are at least ninety percent." She crossed her arms over her chest and shook her head. The obvious chastisement in her gaze made Keller bristle. Only Cassandra could get away with criticizing Chancellor Howyn. Everyone else had to bow their heads and agree. They were at the mercy of his fickle approval.

Howyn stared into her eyes, his expression mutinous. Keller expected him to object, to turn his notorious temper on his beloved daughter. Instead he broke into a reluctant smile. "You have until the end of the week to get your percentages where you want them."

She didn't argue. "I'll keep you informed of my progress."

"I know you will."

Keller released the connection and turned off his vidscreen. What the hell was she working on? He'd been unable to learn the specifics of her current project. No one seemed to know what she was trying to accomplish. Cassie operated outside the currant paradigm. She answered only to her father.

His private audiocom vibrated in his pocket. He removed the tiny device and glanced at the narrow display. General

Bryson? How odd. He pushed the transceiver into his ear. "This better be important."

"I wouldn't have risked the connection if it weren't. We had a situation at site number two. Our guests had to be relocated."

"What sort of situation?"

"I'd rather meet so I can explain in detail."

Keller heaved a frustrated sigh. "Usual place. Give me an hour."

* * * * *

"Renée was remarkably thorough," Fane muttered, mischief gleaming in his eyes. "You'd think she was trying to impress someone."

"That's not funny." Mal Ton crossed his arms over his chest and scowled at his longtime friend.

"According to this report, both the Autumn and Winter Dens are by invitation only. Not even their addresses are available to the public. We have six likely locations, but time is ticking away."

"So how do we get an invitation?" Lorelle asked.

"This is a lot more complicated than sneaking into a condemned building in Old Towne," Fane told her. "Mistress Effie's main club is in the center of the pleasure district. If a Stilox warrior and a human female stroll in and start asking about the Autumn Den, it's going to draw all sorts of attention."

"Mal Ton can shift into whatever we need him to be."

He smiled at her boast. She'd only actually seen him shift once. Still, he appreciated her vote of confidence.

"What about you?" Fane moved out from behind his desk. "You and Mal Ton have certainly spent enough time together. Have you picked up any of his abilities?"

"I don't think so." Her violet gaze darted to Mal Ton for a moment before she looked back at Fane. "Unless you count the language thing."

"A full body shift takes years of practice to master," Mal Ton pointed out. "Maybe she could alter her natural form enough to no long appear human."

"How do I go about that?"

Mal Ton thought for a moment then formed an image in his mind. "The people of Gehinna are warlike. They're popular mercenaries, yet their females are known for their passionate natures. Most importantly, they look very much like humans, except for their coloring." Turning to Lorelle, he pushed his fingers into her hair and lightly circled her temple with his thumb. "Do you see?"

She closed her eyes, accepting the image with absolute trust. Her openness sent warmth swirling through his chest. His mate. She was extraordinary. And it had only taken three hundred years to find her. He smiled and passed affection across their link. He would protect her and surround her with—

"I won't ask when you sampled her DNA," Lorelle interrupted his thoughts with a gentle smile. "I have the image in my mind. What do I do now?"

"Don't attempt an actual shift. Even if you managed to take on her form, you wouldn't be able to maintain it for as long as you'll need the disguise. Concentrate on the color of her skin and the shape of her eyes."

He watched her face, ignoring the impulse to assist her. She needed to figure it out for herself. Her hair darkened first, losing any hint of brown and taking on a faint blue sheen. Next color spread across her smooth skin, faint at first then deepening with a sudden surge.

"Back it off, sweetheart. You're going for a subtle tint not glossy paint."

A quick smile parted her lips then she pressed them together as her concentration turned inward. The sapphire brightness faded, mellowing by degrees until only a powder blue haze remained. Her lips were darker than her skin, taking on a dusky gray-blue shade.

"Very good. Now take several deep breaths and imprint this feeling on your memory."

"I want to see what I look like."

"Not yet. Release the transformation then reform it." As if she'd been performing partial shifts for years, she returned her coloring to normal then recalled the Gehinna hue. "Perfect. Now reshape your eyes and darken the color to match the image I sent you." Her eyelashes took on a midnight blue sheen as they fluttered open. The outer corners of her eyes tilted up and the irises glowed with rich blue fire. "Now you can look at yourself."

"There's a mirror in the bathroom." Fane pointed to a door on her right.

"I still look too much like me." She sounded disappointed and frustrated.

Mal Ton stood in the doorway and studied the result. "You weren't trying to become her. You were trying to mimic her coloring and you've done that beautifully. You are a sensuous, desirable Gehinna female."

"Are you going to turn blue too?" Her teeth appeared especially white framed by her dark blue smile.

"You wouldn't want me to impersonate a Gehinna male. They are true barbarians." He traced her lips with his index finger and lowered his voice. "This color is perfect for your nipples and your pussy. Don't forget to adjust the color of all your hair."

She turned her head and looked into the mirror. "I thought the objective of this transformation was to get us through the door. I have no intention of screwing around at a sex club while Brianna's life hangs in the balance."

He tangled his fingers in the back of her hair. "Look at me." She met his gaze in the mirror instead of turning around. "How far are you willing to go? We already know they're not at the main club. We have to attract the attention of one of the trainers and secure an invitation to the Autumn Den. Brianna's life hangs in the balance. What are you willing to do?"

Lorelle stared at Mal Ton's reflection while uncertainty and dread assailed her calm. Could she bare her body and let strangers touch her? Was she willing to fuck someone to secure Brianna's freedom? Would she fuck more than one?

"It's just sex," she whispered as her insides clenched. "She's my sister. I'll do whatever it takes."

A predatory smile curved his lips and tingles skittered down her spine. "Do you honestly believe I'd let someone else fuck you? There is no way it will go that far."

Her breath released in a thankful whoosh. "But it's likely we'll get naked?"

"Very likely."

"Will the trainers touch us?"

"Possibly."

"Will we be expected to touch them?"

"We won't rush into this blindly." He took her shoulder and guided her around. His other hand still grasped her hair. "We'll understand the rules before we agree to play their games."

"But the more willing we are, the more likely it is that we'll be invited to the next level."

"Yes." His gaze caressed her face, the teal gleaming with warmth and protectiveness.

Fane cleared his throat, reminding them that they weren't alone. "She'll need something to wear. And I need to arrange for backup. You're not going to attempt this alone."

"Who did you have in mind? Max chose these people for a reason. I wouldn't be surprised if many, if not all of the trainers are mutants. Anyone who accompanies us has to be a strong shielder. We don't want our abilities to give us away."

"I'm going to head the other team. I thought I'd take Sean and perhaps one of the other shifters with me."

Mal Ton shook his head. "It's not smart for both of us to go on any mission."

"Smart hasn't gotten us any closer to unmasking Max." Fane waved away his concern and headed for the door. "It's time for rash and reckless."

The door shut behind Fane and Mal Ton turned back to Lorelle. "I know sexuality isn't a weapon you're used to wielding, but we will be all the more convincing because of your vulnerability."

"It will be worth it if—"

He placed his fingers on her lips. "No effort is wasted. Even if we fail or Brianna isn't being held at the Autumn Den we need to do this."

"I know."

His lips brushed over hers and his warm, spicy scent made her tingle. "Pretending to want you is going to be the easiest role I've ever played." He wrapped his arms around her and the distinct ridge of his erection reinforced his claim.

She held him tight and abandoned herself to the kiss. Knowing the stolen moment was destined to pass only made the embrace sweeter.

* * * * *

"Have you ever been to one of my classes before?" Mistress Effie assessed them with wide, heavily lined brown eyes. Her skin bore the bronze tint of a highborn Protarian while the utter perfection of her features hinted at surgical assistance.

"We haven't had the pleasure, but we've heard nothing but rave reviews." Mal Ton's voice rumbled in his chest. He'd followed the same advice he'd given Lorelle and chosen a form not far removed from his natural appearance. The less energy he had to devote to maintaining his shift, the more he could channel into finding the humans.

"Your companion is obviously Gehinna, but your appearance is less distinct. Which races combined to create you?" Her emotions were muted, yet he couldn't be sure if mutant abilities augmented her control or she had simply had years of practice maintaining her composure.

"My mother was Protarian. My father was half Mimossa and half human."

"Human?" She scooted to the edge of her chair and crossed her long, toned legs. "I had never heard of the race until earlier this week."

"Few humans interact with this star system. Perhaps I know your other clients."

A sly smile bowed her pouty lips and still she emanated only faint twinges of emotion. "Information regarding my clients is strictly confidential."

"Of course. I apologize."

"How much do you know about my programs?"

"This is a training facility not an entertainment club. Each exercise has been designed with a specific purpose." He glanced at Lorelle to see how she was holding up. She sat beside him, her deep blue gaze fixed on Mistress Effie. Her emotions were so carefully guarded he had to touch her mind to assure himself she was all right.

She glanced at him, obviously sensing his increased presence in her mind. *The faster we pass inspection, the sooner we can start earning an invitation to the Autumn Den.* Her telepathic response was tentative even though he'd assured her their private link was well shielded.

"I need to know a bit about you." Mistress Effie's gaze narrowed just a bit. Had she sensed Lorelle's transmission or was she just responding to the sudden hush? "It's important that I place you in the program that will benefit you the most."

"The application was detailed. What else do you need to know?" With so little time to plan, they'd had to keep their story generic. He didn't want to suggest a situation she would attempt to verify.

"How did you meet?" she addressed the question to Lorelle.

"I danced in a bar." Lorelle shrugged, appearing bored and indifferent. "He enjoyed my act and was less obnoxious than most of the guys, so we eventually got together. This is his idea not mine. I don't need some namby-pamby school teaching me how to fuck."

Mistress Effie chuckled, eyeing Lorelle with more interest. "What about him? Perhaps his skills could use some refining."

"If you saw the size of his dick, you'd understand why this is a waste of time."

"Is a large penis all it takes to satisfy you?"

"It sure as hell doesn't hurt."

Mistress Effie turned back to Mal Ton. "Why did you bring her here?"

"She's impatient. She has the most amazing body, but she won't let me enjoy it. As soon as she gets wet, she wants me to shove it in and get it over with."

"Fascinating." She turned back to Lorelle. "How often do you orgasm?"

"Often enough. Fucking is fucking. Insert tab A into slot B and slide back and forth. I don't need a *trainer* to tell me that!"

Mal Ton made a distressed sound and swept his hand toward Lorelle. "You see the problem? She has no idea what she's missing."

"Have you ever tied her up?"

"I've been tempted, but she can be a real hellion when she's riled."

Lorelle scoffed, slapping her knee with one hand. "It would take more than one man to tie me up."

"That shouldn't be a problem." Mistress Effie stood and smiled down at Lorelle. "You're lucky your lover understands that there is far more to fucking than you've allowed him to demonstrate." Mistress Effie depressed a trigger on the control pad strapped to her wrist then looked at Mal Ton. "Are you ready?"

"I can't wait to begin."

A door on the far side of the reception area slid open and two tall, burly men stepped into the room.

"Escort this couple to training room three and prepare the female for Master Amadi."

Mal Ton stood and held out his hand toward Lorelle. *Great job, sweetheart.* The uncertainty in her gaze increased his need to touch her. He slipped his arm around her waist as they followed their escorts into the corridor. *We're on our way.*

On our way to what? Lorelle carefully hid the thought from Mal Ton. The roles they'd devised gave her an outlet for her anxiety. She could argue and resist without seeming suspicious. Still, she didn't want Mal Ton to realize how disconcerting she found the situation. The more turbulent her emotions became the harder it would be for her to hold the shift. She was far more comfortable with overt aggression than deception.

Fane and his team were monitoring the situation. At the first hint of danger they'd storm the facility and rush Mal Ton and Lorelle to safety. Mal Ton had assured her they wouldn't actually watch, but she wasn't sure it mattered. They all knew what was going on inside the training center.

One of Effie's thugs opened a door and motioned them inside. No sooner had they entered the room than the other brute grabbed her upper arms.

"Get your paws off me!" A slow, taunting smile was his only response as she jerked against his restraining hands.

"We are only here to assist you, sir," Thug One told Mal Ton.

"Good. It distresses me to see others handling my female." Thug Two held her arms so she kicked out at Mal Ton. "Stop that. It will do no good to fight us. You brought this on yourself."

She gasped. "How do you figure that?"

His current appearance was far less striking than his natural shape, which was the main reason he'd chosen the form. Brown hair flowed away from his face in wide waves. He was shorter now, his build stocky as opposed to fluidly muscled. Mutant fire flashed for an instant within his light brown eyes.

"I've tried to show you the pleasures waiting us beyond basic fucking. You won't allow me to be creative." His deft fingers unbuttoned the front of her blouse and parted the sides, revealing her simple undergarment. "You are capable of so much more. I'm no longer willing to be compromised by your impatience." He rubbed his thumbs over her nipples, watching them tighten beneath the clingy fabric of her undershirt.

Her ragged breathing increased the pressure of his thumbs and heightened the sensations created by his light caress. "I'll slow down, I promise. You don't need to tie me up."

He chuckled and shifted his gaze to the fastenings at the front of her pants. "It's too late for compromises, love. You are going to be trained." Thug One removed her shoes while Mal Ton pulled off her pants. She twisted and kicked, but the men easily avoided her flailing feet. "This will probably take all three of us." Mal Ton drew her undershirt up and Thug One pulled it off over her head. She jerked one arm free and launched herself forward. Mal Ton caught her and pressed her back into Thug One's waiting hands. Her panties soon followed and the thugs dragged her backward.

She couldn't see where they were taking her, but the lustful gleam in Mal Ton's eyes made her renew her struggles.

"They won't hurt you if you stop fighting them." Mal Ton matched them step for step, his hot gaze every bit as tangible as their hands.

"They won't hurt her unless they're ordered to," the deep male voice drew her attention to the doorway.

"Master," the thugs greeted in unison.

Amadi had a boyish charm that seemed incongruous with his title. Wildly curling blond hair framed his handsome face. Prominent cheekbones and a straight nose led her gaze to his mouth. His bottom lip was fuller than the top and dimples added to his youthful appeal.

"Carry on," he told the thugs, amusement dancing in his baby blue eyes. "Mistress Effie warned me this would require all my skills."

Lorelle forgot her sarcastic response as Thug One pivoted and she saw their destination. It looked like an oversized shower base—except for the shackles! She wiggled and yelled, kicking out at Thug Two.

"I'd heard Gehinna women were spirited." Amadi stood beside Mal Ton, obviously enjoying the show. "Is she always like this?"

"You have no idea."

Thug One closed a shackle around her wrist with an intimidating snap while Thug Two wrestled her feet into position. As soon as her arms were secured above her head, Thug One bound her ankles. Her legs were drawn apart until her body was open and helpless. Her breath caught in her throat as she waited for them to take advantage of her obscene position.

"Will there be anything else?" Thug One asked Amadi, and Lorelle exhaled.

"Not right now. Thank you."

Emboldened by their departure, Lorelle tugged against one side and then the other. "This isn't funny! Open these things right now." She sent a fresh wave of energy through her body, reinforcing her shift.

"Undress and join her," Amadi directed.

Mal Ton immediately moved to obey. Lorelle turned the full force of her indignation on Amadi. "You perverted little prick! I won't stand for this."

In an instant, his humor evaporated and his gaze turned to ice. He approached her with purposeful steps and curved his fingers around her chin. "You agreed to acquire these skills when you signed your application. Disobedience will be punished and cooperation rewarded. You are now involved in a barter where the only commodity is pleasure. You will receive pleasure thankfully and give pleasure without hesitation. Do you understand?"

"I understand that you're deluded. Unfasten these cuffs!"

Mal Ton moved up beside Amadi and possessively cupped her breast. Despite his altered appearance, she recognized the unyielding intensity of his gaze. "This has been a long time coming, sweetheart. The sooner you surrender and allow yourself to learn, the sooner we can move on to other lessons." He looked at Amadi while his hand subtlety staked his claim. "How would you like me to begin?"

Amadi stepped back and motioned toward the wall. "Turn on the sprayer and wet her down. Each session starts with a shower. This relaxes everyone and establishes intimacy. Until your female is willing to cooperate, you'll have to bathe her."

"Not a problem." Mal Ton reached behind her and activated the shower.

Warm water streamed out of a handheld sprayer. She refocused her mind as he rinsed his body, but all too soon his attention shifted to her. After saturating her hair, he teased her breasts. Tiny jets of water simulated her nipples and areolas as he moved the sprayer in a circular pattern.

"That's enough!" Her nipples puckered and tingles trailed across her skin congregating between her thighs. She arched away, but he simply followed her movements with the sprayer. "I showered this morning."

"Relax, love. That's what this is all about. Your body is capable of so much more than you've allowed yourself to feel."

"Lorelle will be the focus of this first session. Do you have any objections?"

"Not at all." Mal Ton continued to arouse her with the sprayer. "That's why I brought her here."

"I object! There is nothing wrong with—" Amadi pinched her nipple just hard enough to make her gasp.

"You cannot learn until you open your mind to new experiences."

Mal Ton swept the water up and down her torso, reaching lower with each pass. Lorelle clenched her teeth and turned her face to the side. Should she fight the sensations or let herself come? Could she maintain her shift while her body spiraled out of control? Mal Ton wasn't giving her much choice.

The tiny jets pulsed against her clit for just a second then Mal Ton angled the water lower, tantalizing her folds with the liquid rush. She moaned, instinctively tightening her inner muscles against the sensual barrage.

"You're tensing." Amadi rolled one of her nipples between his thumb and forefinger. She glanced at him and realized the significance of the caress. If she didn't relax and accept the stimulation, he'd pinch her again.

"Does the lesson end when I come?"

"No. But you'll be one step closer to freedom." He took the sprayer from Mal Ton's hand. "Caress her for as long as you like. She has no choice but to accept your touch."

Turning to the wall dispenser, he coated his palms then slid his soapy hands down one of her upraised arms, across her chest and up the other side. She shivered and goose bumps broke out across her skin.

Mal Ton eased into her mind, soothing her anxiety and reinforcing her shift while his hands worshiped her body. Amadi warmed her legs with the sprayer while Mal Ton explored her torso. His slippery hands glided across her breasts and over her shoulders, never staying in one place for long.

Desire uncoiled within her, making her head spin. Her nipples heated and her pussy melted, anticipating his next move. He circled her slowly, dragging his fingertips across her ribs then down her spine and into the crack between her ass cheeks.

"You are so beautiful." Mal Ton's voice hitched and his rough tone made her heart flutter. He followed her deep crease into the warmth between her thighs. His fingers brushed across her folds as he cupped her breast with the other hand.

"Tease her any way you like," Amadi coached, "but don't give her your cock. She has to earn that privilege."

Insolent pup. Does he really think he knows more than I do about giving you pleasure? His fingers gently parted her folds while his thumb slid back and pressed against her anus. Open, waiting yet denied, her body longed for penetration.

Aubrey Ross

Just play along. She could scarcely think beyond the throbbing he accented. *He doesn't know who you are.*

Mal Ton circled her opening twice then removed his hand from between her thighs. She wiggled back against him, trying to recapture the caress. Instead he rubbed against her back and cupped her breasts with both hands. His cock pressed lengthwise into her bottom crease, the thick shaft an undeniable promise of the pleasures awaiting her.

"Do you feel that?" Passion made his voice harsh and hoarse.

"Give it to me. Fuck me hard while I'm still chained like this." The urgency in her voice was genuine. She'd had no idea how stimulating helplessness could be.

He plucked her nipples and rocked against her while his teeth scraped the side of her neck. Amadi ceased to exist. The room fell away until all she felt was Mal Ton and the demanding emptiness of her own body.

"Are you willing to obey?" Mal Ton rolled her nipples, pushing the sensation right to the trembling edge of pain.

"Yes. Fuck me now and I'll do whatever you say."

He chuckled and covered her breasts with his palms, abrading her sensitive nipples with his palms. "Closer, but not good enough." He pulled back and bent his knees. Hot and hard, his shaft slid between her legs, parting her folds until he came to rest against her entrance.

She shivered. Her hands clenched tight and her core pulsed, empty and eager for his fullness. His mouth opened against the side of her neck, electrifying her senses with firm suction and tender nips.

Amadi swept the water from hip to hip then targeted her clit with a slow up and down motion. Prickly sensations gathered in her pussy. She squeezed her eyes shut and concentrated on maintaining the changes in her appearance. Mal Ton moved his arm to circle her waist. More of his energy flowed into her, calming her and stabilizing her shift.

She relaxed against him, welcoming the rush of heat and escalating tension. The first flutters of her orgasm rippled through her core and Amadi pulled the sprayer back.

"What did I do wrong?" she cried as the pleasure dissipated. "I thought you wanted me to come."

"I'm not your Master. Your orgasms belong to him."

"Then tell him to fuck me! This is cruel."

With his arm still banding her waist and his cock throbbing between her thighs, Mal Ton reached down with his free hand and carefully pulled on her swollen clit. Pleasure burst so suddenly Lorelle screamed. Hard, clenching spasms gripped her body and her knees buckled.

For a breathless instant nothing existed but the pleasure. Reality dimmed as she trembled in his arms. His clever fingers prolonged the sensations and lights danced before her eyes.

Sweet, possessive passion flowed into her mind. The thread of smug satisfaction made her smile. He was good and he knew it. She couldn't really blame him for his arrogance when her body was still tingling from a staggering release.

A warm chuckle drew her back from the velvet lethargy. "You have some skill, I see." Amadi crossed his arms over his chest and looked at Mal Ton with renewed interest. "Her response was reluctant yet powerful and you are obviously ready for our intermediate class."

She felt Mal Ton stiffen against her back. *Intermediate class? I should be training the trainers.*

This isn't about you, my love. Reinforce your role.

A telepathic grumble was his only response.

"I'm supposed to lead a group session at the Autumn Den this afternoon. Would you be interested in accompanying me?"

Lorelle licked her lips and tried not to react to the offer. Could it really be this easy?

It's too damn easy. Mal Ton echoed her concern. *But I don't see that we have a choice.* He stepped out from behind her as Amadi turned off the sprayer. "I'm too possessive for a group session."

"Client interaction is strictly voluntary. No one will touch her but you or me if I felt something needed to be demonstrated. Somehow I don't think that will be a problem."

"I'm not sure she's ready for more. Maybe we better stick with—"

"She's ready. None of the other trainers will allow you to advance this quickly. You can ride with me to the other facility and we'll continue our lesson."

Mal Ton's shoulders tensed, but his expression didn't change. "I'd prefer to meet you there. I think we need to talk about what's happened so far."

"She doesn't need to talk, she needs to feel. If we don't continue, our progress will be lost."

"What about our ship?"

"Someone will shuttle you back after the session."

Pausing for a long introspective moment, Mal Ton finally nodded. "We can't break through her defenses if I'm not willing to trust you."

"Good. I'll let Mistress Effie know there's been a change of plans." He opened a compartment in the adjacent wall and tossed Mal Ton a set of simple handcuffs. "You may dress, but I want her to remain naked."

"I am not parading around naked!"

"You will do whatever your Master wishes you to do. I had intended on bringing you a cloak, but I'll leave the decision up to him. Do you need assistance preparing her?"

"No. We'll be ready when you return."

Amadi's gaze lingered on Lorelle for a moment then he left the room.

Chapter Nine

ဢ

Every instinct in Keller's suspicious nature jarred to high alert as General Bryson stepped out of the nondescript shuttle. Bryson had been Chancellor Howyn's henchman for far too long for Keller to take his defection seriously. The clearing was barely discernable from the air. Without exact coordinates and a reason to look, no one would notice two random ships well away from the bustling heart of Sanctum.

Bryson blamed his change of heart on Howyn's ruthless use of one of his lesser wives and the chancellor's continual refusal to reward his years of loyalty. The motivation was believable enough. Still, Keller couldn't silence his qualms.

"What was so important?" Keller demanded. "Howyn is watching me like a hawk."

The general's brow arched in response to the statement. "He's more suspicious than you realize, *Max*."

Keller grabbed his upper arm and sneered. "Shut the fuck up. Someone could have followed me."

"Then you're not half as clever as you claim." Bryson jerked his arm out of Keller's grasp and smiled. "I just helped evacuate the old Pirautial estate."

"*What?*" He raked his hair with both hands as tension twisted through his gut. "How did Howyn find them?"

"Your guess is as good as mine. Bribed one of your guards? Followed someone who wasn't paying attention? Take your pick."

This couldn't be happening. First Fane and Mal Ton snatch the most promising humans right out from under his nose and now he'd lost three more to Howyn. "Where did you take them?"

"That's the really wonderful part." Bryson pulled on the sleeve of his shirt, looking out of place in civilian clothing. "Howyn's private guard took off with our reluctant guests and said not a word to me. The only reason Howyn had me there was to rub my face in how far I've fallen. A few weeks ago I would have led the raid."

"Goddamn it!" Keller kicked at the dirt, a poor substitute for the violent images dancing through his imagination. "Has he figured out who I am?"

"If he hasn't, it's only a matter of time. Can any of those women identify you?"

He shook his head. "The only two who saw my face are with Effie."

"I say you cut your losses before this crashes down around both of us. Howyn has what he needs. You've lost your bargaining power."

Nothing had gone right since he'd decided to make his move against Fane. His attack on Howyn's transport had been meant to force the ship to land, not crash it into the side of a mountain. Both Howyn and Fane had humans now. Bryson was right. It was time for a new strategy.

"If you're going to have contact with them—even if it's only long enough to dispose of them—you'll need one of these." Bryson held out an injector.

"What is it?"

"I'm not exactly sure. All I know is Howyn had everyone who went on the mission inoculated before we left and the women were inoculated before they were moved. Something about human physiology interfering with the counteragent."

He took the injector out of Bryson's hand and studied the elongated cylinder as his suspicion mounted. Howyn had no access to the humans until today. How would he have known about this supposed interference much less formulated a cure *before* the raid?

Keller put the injector in his pocket. "Do you have more than one?"

"Why?"

"There are others on my team who will need it."

Keller watched the general closely, searching for any sign of deception.

"Doctor Myer gave me a fistful of them. You're welcome to what was left." A calculative gleam flashed in his gaze as he turned toward his shuttle.

Doctor Myer! Of course Cassie was right in the middle of this. But was she preventing another epidemic or doing her father's dirty work?

* * * * *

Mal Ton pulled on his pants and boots before he approached Lorelle. *They're probably watching us, so don't be too cooperative.*

"I hate you," she said while her blue gaze caressed his face.

"Shall I fuck you before we leave?" He cupped the back of her neck with one hand and covered her sex with the other. "I don't think all this is water." He slipped his middle finger between her slick folds. "I should have restrained you weeks ago. I had no idea how much you would like it."

He pressed his mouth over hers, using the kiss to conceal their telepathic communication. *There's no doubt this is a trap. Fane will follow us to the Autumn Den, but we can't reveal ourselves until we have the humans in sight.*

How will Fane know what's going on? What if they don't take us out through the main entrance? She wiggled and moaned, her inner muscles snug around his finger.

Fane knows already. He gentled the kiss and saturated her being with energy. *Your skin keeps flushing pink as your excitement mounts. A true Gehinna's skin deepens to smoky blue. If you can't manage that, just maintain one color.*

Stop turning me on. He pulled back and she used her hair to hide her smile.

Easier said than done when I want you this *badly.* He rubbed against her to demonstrate.

Through sheer force of will, he reined in his desire and took her face between his hands. "You are mine to enjoy any way I want. You will obey or suffer the consequences."

Her chin came up at his autocratic tone then understanding calmed her sudden surge of anger. "Just because you get me hot doesn't mean you own me. Don't let this go to your head. Men line up for the chance to fuck a full-blooded Gehinna. I can replace you with the snap of my fingers."

"If you don't adjust your attitude soon, you'll be putting that claim to the test." He unfastened the shower restraint from around one of her wrists and replaced it with the handcuff. With quick, intentional movements, he freed her other wrist and drew her hands together in front of her. Before she could cause trouble, he pushed her to her knees. "I want your word that you'll not try to escape and you'll cooperate until the afternoon session ends."

She raised her bound hands and glared at him. "What choice do I have?"

"I know you better than that. You could work your way out of those cuffs and head out the door almost as fast as I could. I don't want to force this on you. I want you to give it a chance."

"Fine," she huffed out the word, and averted her face.

"That didn't sound very sincere. Try again."

"I promise to obey you—for today only."

146

"All right. Lean forward." After a tense pause she lowered her hands to the floor and flipped her hair out of her face, watching his approach. Her ankles were still connected to the shower base, opening her, offering her most intimate flesh for his pleasure. He stepped down into the shower area and traced a path from her nape to the crack between her ass cheeks. Pausing to explore one silky curve, he eventually worked his way into her warm folds. "You're still hot and damp. Shall I fuck you with my fingers?"

"Whatever pleases you." Sarcasm made her voice sound brittle.

Where the hell was their illustrious trainer? Mal Ton wanted Amadi to walk in before this got too far. He slowly pushed his middle finger into her pussy. A shiver passed down his spine as her inner muscles embraced him. "Are you this hot for any man, or do you want me as much as I want you?"

"Any long, hard cock will get the job done. Yours just happens to be longer and harder than most."

Jealous hunger surged within him and Mal Ton gritted his teeth. She was playing her part, nothing more. What was wrong with him? He added a second finger and thrust faster, determined to ignore the pressure building in his groin.

The door slid open so he brought his hand down across her ass. "You will crave my cock and only my cock or you will never come again!"

Amadi grabbed Mal Ton's wrist as he prepared to spank her again. "Punishment is a useful motivation when she has earned it. It is your responsibility to make her crave your cock. By putting her pleasure above your own you will show her that you are the only man who can satisfy her. Threats are seldom effective."

Mal Ton pulled his fingers out of her body and inhaled her tantalizing scent. "You're right. It's just that she has tormented me for so long."

"You are both here now. That's an important first step." He moved in front of Lorelle and raised her face. "I know you enjoy fucking him. Is lust all you feel when he's inside you?"

"It doesn't matter." Her lashes swept down, hiding her expression. "He'll leave me. They always do. He'll get tired of the novelty and…"

"I understand."

The vulnerability in her tone tugged at Mal Ton's heart. Even knowing she was only acting, he wanted to wrap his arms around her and assure her he would never leave. He gave himself a firm mental shake. This conflict was meant to distract Amadi. Mal Ton didn't sense mutant energy radiating from the younger man, but there was a slim possibility his mental shields were impenetrable.

Mal Ton folded his arms over his chest and immersed himself in his role. "Does dishonesty warrant punishment?"

Amadi dragged his gaze away from Lorelle and asked, "Is she being dishonest?"

"She's a cock tease. She makes men so hot they'll kill each other for one night in her bed. But her partners don't leave her. She leaves them."

"Let's continue this conversation on the ship. I really do need to get going."

Amadi unfastened Lorelle's ankles and draped a long, hooded cloak around her shoulders while Mal Ton finished dressing. As they made their way to the rooftop shuttle lot, Mal Ton opened his mind to Fane. Rather than risking a lengthy explanation, he allowed Fane to scan his consciousness. A driving sense of purpose inundated Mal Ton's empathic receptors a moment later. Fane understood the plan and was anxious to act.

The shuttle was largely automated. After a quick departure check, Amadi entered their destination into the navigation computer and turned to face his guests.

"How long will it take to reach this other location?" Mal Ton didn't have to feign impatience. He'd had enough of Amadi's superiority. This little bastard likely knew who Max was and his current location. Mal Ton wanted to release his shift and shake Amadi until the answers came tumbling out.

"We have plenty of time to explore the source of your frustration." Amadi folded his hands in his lap and crossed his legs. "How long have you two been a couple?"

"I thought you were going to teach us how to have better sex, not psychoanalyze us."

Lorelle sat beside Mal Ton, holding the cloak together with both hands. Her expression gave nothing away, but anxiety pulsed beneath her calm exterior. *If you keep him talking maybe we won't have to perform anymore.*

Lust blasted Mal Ton every time Amadi looked at Lorelle, so he suspected the trainer would find another reason for her to "perform". *I won't let him touch you. Even if I have to end this charade early, he's not touching you.*

"I'm just trying to understand the dynamics of your relationship. True intimacy begins in the mind. If you have unresolved issues between you, your sex life will suffer."

"We both have complicated pasts," Lorelle said. "One of the things I like most about him is his willingness to leave it alone. I'm with him now and nothing else matters."

"Nothing else matters as long as we both make different choices. If we don't learn from our mistakes nothing will ever change."

"Very true." Amadi's gaze settled on Lorelle and he slowly licked his lips. "Are you ready to share yourself with only one man?"

"I wouldn't be here if I didn't want to make this work. But it's harder than I thought it would be. What he said is partly true. I end relationships as soon as I sense a man's interest starting to wane. But I only do so to make it easier on myself. I've been fucked and disregarded more times than you can imagine. Men only want one thing from me."

"I want more than your amazing body." Mal Ton reached over and took her hand. "I enjoy spending time with you and hearing you laugh. Even our arguments are invigorating as long as we don't allow them to go too far."

She squeezed his fingers and tenderness rushed across their private link. "I want to believe that so badly."

Amadi glanced at the control console before offering them his attention again. "I had planned on a quick demonstration in punishment, but I think something different might be more beneficial. Words are easy to disregard. I want you each to show the other how you feel about them. The point of this exercise is to heighten sensations and deepen your emotional connection, so neither of you has permission to come."

Sizzling anticipation assailed Mal Ton from all sides. Despite the circumstance, Lorelle was hungry for his embrace and Amadi wanted to watch them, drawing pleasure from their uninhibited exchange.

Mal Ton took Lorelle by the hand and drew her between his legs. Her long cloak hid them from view and he was curious to see how long Amadi would allow the arrangement. Sliding his hands up the back of her legs, Mal Ton cupped her firm bottom. She smiled and placed her hands on his shoulders as she bent down to kiss him. The kiss was slow and deep. Passion and affection flowed freely across their link, connecting them on a level Amadi would never understand.

"He gave you pleasure before," Amadi reminded. "Show him your appreciation."

He wants me to suck you off. She knelt on the floor and reached for the fastenings at the front of his pants. *Why do you think that is?*

Watching those soft lips slide up and down my cock will make it all the easier for him to imagine himself in my place.

He can imagine all he likes. My mouth belongs to you.

Joy surged through Mal Ton, warm and intoxicating. He pressed his hand against the side of her face and paused for another lingering kiss.

Her deft fingers found his erection and drew it out. Annoyed by the confines of the bunched material, he lifted his hips and pushed his pants to his knees. She pumped him firmly as she stared into his eyes, dragging her fist from tip to root with long, curving strokes.

Amadi left the pilot's chair, moving from position to position until he found the angle that provided the best view. She closed her lips around the flared head of Mal Ton's cock, preventing Amadi from seeing exactly what she was doing. She swirled her tongue over the top and explored the tiny hole until Mal Ton growled and grabbed the back of her hair.

"Slide slowly." His throaty tone brooked no refusal.

She sucked him into her mouth, her lips firm against his throbbing shaft. Heat swept through him, igniting sensations as the wave coalesced between his thighs. She drew back, her tongue seeking out the places that made his breath hitch and his head spin. Up and down, deeper and faster until his balls ached and his chest burned.

"If I don't get to come, you better stop."

Pausing with just his cock head in her mouth, she met his gaze. Her lips sucked and her tongue swirled, her farewell identical to her welcome. "I think the thank you would have meant a lot more without that stipulation."

"Perhaps." Amadi adjusted his pants and returned to the pilot's chair. "He won't have long to wait for the rest. We're almost there."

Mal Ton refastened his pants and took several deep breaths. Lorelle overlapped the cloak and held it closed as she returned to her seat.

You look a little flushed, sweetheart. Try to calm down.

151

Calm down? A sharp laugh accompanied her question. *I'm ready to impale myself on you and I don't care who sees us. God I ache.*

We'll take care of that ache as soon as we free the others.

Shame sparked within her shimmering gaze and she blew out a ragged breath. "How many people are in each session? Will they all be couples or do some people seek out this sort of training on their own?"

"I'm not sure who's scheduled to attend." Amadi faced the control panel as they neared their destination. "We'll find out soon enough."

The shuttle lot was situated behind a drab building. There was nothing on the exterior to indicate what the building housed.

Incapacitate him as soon as he sets down, Fane instructed. *Don't let him alert the others to your arrival.*

Mal Ton released the shift, rolling his shoulders as his natural shape immerged. The shuttle rocked several times then came to rest with a muffled hiss. He moved into Amadi's peripheral vision and the trainer jerked his head toward Mal Ton. With one well-placed punch he rendered Amadi unconscious. Lorelle found the control for the hatch as he powered down the shuttle.

"I like your outfit." Fane grinned at Lorelle as he climbed aboard. She just shook her head, refusing to rise to the bait. "It's a simple setup. One large room flanked by three smaller rooms on each side. There are four Protarians congregated in one of the smaller rooms. Our targets are in the farthest room back on the opposite side."

"You can sense all that?" Lorelle asked.

Fane chuckled. "Sorry to disappoint you. Our ship has scanners."

Lorelle released her shift as well. Mal Ton found her natural shape even more desirable than her previous form, but he could let nothing distract him from the mission.

"How do we want to play this?" Mal Ton worked one of Amadi's arms out of his sleeve as he waited for Fane to answer.

"Shift into Amadi and drag me inside," Lorelle suggested. "We'll tell them you took off and Amadi can insist I be locked in with the others until Max can decide what to do with me."

"We don't know for certain that Amadi knows about Max." Mal Ton pulled the shirt over Amadi's head.

"He knows." Fane took the shirt from Mal Ton and handed it to Lorelle. "I got a peek at his mind right before you knocked him out. He was going to have the other trainers waiting for you when you walked through the door. That's why I broke telepathic silence and warned you."

"Thank you."

Fane politely turned his back as Mal Ton released one side of the handcuffs. She donned the shirt and he refastened the cuffs. The shirt only came to mid-thigh and her nipples were clearly visible through the fabric. Still, it offered her some semblance of modesty. With Mal Ton's assistance, she swung the cloak back onto her shoulders and tied the velvet cords.

"You didn't happen to bring a pulse pistol, did you?" she asked Fane. "Even with the element of surprise on our side, the odds are still in their favor."

"They might scan for munitions," Fane told her. "It's better if you get us inside. Sean will be on your heels and I'll be in as soon as the action starts."

"It will likely be over before you figure out another way in." Fane didn't argue, so Mal Ton laid his hand on Amadi's shoulder and closed his eyes.

"Disproportionate mass complicates any shift," Fane leaned down and whispered in her ear. "It takes more energy and a higher level of concentration for Mal Ton to reshape his body into a smaller form. The trainer is a good head shorter than Mal Ton."

The shift passed over his body, rolling from his feet to his head in a smooth, sustained wave. His true appearance was swept away and Amadi formed in its place. No matter how many times she watched it happen, she was awed by his power.

"Ready?" he asked, his voice transforming as well.

"Absolutely." He swept his hand toward the hatchway. "How resistant should I be?"

"How resistant would you be if Mal Ton sensed danger and took off, leaving you with Amadi?"

"You would never run from a fight."

"They don't know that." Mal Ton wrapped his fingers around her forearm and led her off the shuttle. As they neared the building, she began to resist. Tugging against his hold and digging in her heels as much as her bare feet allowed.

He stepped onto a square pad in front of the door, triggering a full-body scanner. Lorelle held her breath as the scanner analyzed the accuracy of Mal Ton's shift. The door hissed open a moment later and she released her pent-up breath.

You need to try to hurt me, sweetheart, or no one is going to believe us. She kicked his thigh and jerked away violently, only to turn and swing her hands at his face. *Much more like it.* He caught her upper arm and shoved her into the building.

"He'll be back for me, you depraved prick! Don't you dare lay a hand on me."

"If you're so important to him, why'd he take off without you?" She swung for his face again. Mal Ton caught her around the waist and pushed her up against the wall with enough force to make her grunt. "Hit me again, you bloodthirsty bitch, and I'll hit you back!"

Three men and a woman rushed out of the office not far from where they were standing. "What's going on?" a tall blond man asked. "We were told you were bringing us a man and a female Gehinna."

"Yeah that's what I thought too. They both shapeshifted and the man took off as soon as I opened the hatch. He must have realized it was a trap."

"Did you recognize him?"

"No, but they're obviously mutants. What should we do with her?"

A dark-haired man shouldered the blond aside. "She looks human. Are you sure she shifted?"

Mal Ton rolled his eyes. "Shifting is a little hard to misunderstand when it happens right in front of you."

"We have to notify —"

"No names," the blond cut in.

"Put her in with the others," the lone woman said. "Regardless of her species, it's the safest place for her. I'll comm 'our leader'. After what happened this morning he's sure to be in a shitty mood."

Grabbing Lorelle by the upper arm, Mal Ton propelled her forward. "I hope you need to be interrogated. I can't remember the last time anyone has gotten me this hard."

The others snickered at the taunt and they quickly crossed the main room. Unlike the Summer Den there were no sexual apparatus displayed in the common room. With its gleaming wood floor and clean lines, it reminded Lorelle of a martial arts dojo.

Time slowed as they neared the final door on the left side of the room. The blond scanned open the door and Mal Ton released her arm. In one sustained motion, Mal Ton shifted and pounced on the blond, pummeling him with fast, vicious strikes.

Lorelle spun and kicked hard, catching the man behind her squarely in the gut. He bent over with a startled groan, both arms wrapped around his middle. She clasped her bound hands together and slammed them against the back of his head. He sprawled in an unconscious heap at her feet.

Sean materialized behind the dark-haired man. A sizzling blast from a pulse pistol streaked past his head as he rammed his shoulder into the trainer's side. Lorelle's gaze darted to the female trainer who was rushing across the floor, gun in hand.

Having incapacitated the blond, Mal Ton dove for the woman as she adjusted her aim and fired again. Mal Ton struck her wrist with his forearm, sending the shot into the floor. She spit out a curse and turned on Mal Ton. They struggled a moment longer before he snatched the weapon out of her hand.

"On your stomach, hands behind your head," he shouted.

Sean was still grappling with the last of Max's men. Lorelle took a step toward them then caught sight of Fane coming out of one of the adjoining rooms. He sprinted toward Sean, more than ready to help.

She didn't stop to ponder how he'd gotten in. With Max's people more or less subdued, she turned toward the door. A blonde woman peeked out, her gaze huge and watchful. Lorelle recognized her from the transport but couldn't remember her name. Was Brianna in there too? Lorelle's pulse raced and her mouth went dry as she hurried toward the door. The blonde recoiled and Lorelle held up both hands.

"I'm not going to hurt you. We've come to get you out of here." The blonde drew back her hand and the door started to close. Lorelle lunged forward and caught the door an instant before it shut. She pushed inward but remained in the doorway. The blonde stood in the corner with her arms wrapped around a dark-haired woman. "Brianna?"

Both women looked up, but Lorelle's heart fell as she saw the other woman's face.

"You were on... I remember you from the ship," the brunette said.

"My name is Lorelle. Do you know where they took my sister?" They both shook their heads and tears stung Lorelle's eyes. *You're being a selfish bitch!* These women were just as

156

worthy of rescue as Brianna. She shook off her disappointment and tossed her cloak to the blonde. "Wrap that around you both for now. We'll find something for you to wear."

"Why are you handcuffed?" the blonde asked.

Lorelle glanced at her hands and smiled. "It's a long story."

Chapter Ten

Lorelle stood beside Donna as Fane spoke with the bedraggled blonde. An occasional flicker of mutant light told her he was scanning her mind as well as asking her questions. The brunette's name was Kylie, but Lorelle knew little else about the woman. Donna hovered over her like a protective mother, agreeing to tell them anything they wanted to know if they left Kylie alone.

"We were given injections yesterday," Donna told Fane. "Most of our symptoms subsided within a few hours."

"Most, not all?"

She shrugged, fiddling with her sleeve. Mal Ton had found simple, adjustable garments stacked in one of the smaller training rooms. "Kylie still has headaches and I'm having really strange dreams. What are you going to do with *them*?" She pointed toward the cell from which she'd been released.

"We haven't decided yet."

Donna looked at Lorelle and managed to smile. "I'm sorry about your sister. I hope she's all right."

"So do I."

"Did you only see the leader on the night your ship crashed?" Fane persisted.

"Yeah, but I saw him clearly. I bet I can pick him out of a lineup or whatever."

"I have a pretty good idea who he is, but I'd be thankful if you confirmed his identity for me."

He made it sound like one more moderately important detail. Lorelle knew he'd been attempting to confirm Max's identity for weeks.

"He's hard to describe. There's nothing remarkable about his appearance."

"If you form a clear image of him in your mind, I'll be able to see it."

"You can read minds?" Donna's gaze filled with suspicion then darted to Lorelle.

"It's all right," she assured. "He's one of the good guys."

Fane didn't even need to touch her. Donna formed the image and he muttered a string of Protarian curses that made Lorelle smile.

"What's wrong?" Mal Ton slipped his arm around Lorelle's waist as he reached the small group.

"Donna just confirmed Max's identity," Lorelle told him.

"Why is that a bad thing?"

"We were right," Fane rubbed his eyes with his fingertips. "Max is Howyn's pet mutant."

"That can't surprise you. I know you've had specters following him ever since he returned to Protaria."

Fane looked pointedly at Donna then changed the subject. "Ostan should look them over and Andrea will want blood samples before we turn them loose."

"Turn us loose?" Donna sounded painfully hopeful. "Are you able to take us back to Earth?"

"Perhaps," Mal Ton said, "if that's still where you want to go once you understand the situation."

Fane told Sean to take the women out to the shuttle. Mal Ton squeezed her side, assuring her the directives had only been meant for Donna and Kylie.

"Do we just leave the trainers here for someone to find?" She wasn't sure why they were still loitering in the main room of the Autumn Den.

"According to the female trainer, Max is about half an hour out."

"Max is on his way here?" Fane crossed his arms over his chest and scowled.

"That's what the female said and a gun was pressed to her head at the time." Mutant intensity glimmered in Mal Ton's gaze. "She seemed sincere to me."

"I'd like nothing better than to drag him back to headquarters in restraints, but we both know it's impossible."

"Why is it impossible?" Lorelle pushed Mal Ton's hand off her hip and faced him. "He knows where Brianna is. I say we hang around and beat it out of him."

"It's not that simple. He—"

As if to prove Mal Ton's point, a dark-haired man in a business suit flashed into view. He didn't materialize like a specter. One moment there were three people standing in the common room and the next there were four.

"Well, this is awkward." The stranger flicked a piece of lint off his sleeve, obviously unimpressed by either Mal Ton or Fane.

Mal Ton pivoted on the balls of his feet and pushed Lorelle behind him. "Where are the other females, Keller? This has gone on long enough."

"Isn't this Max?" Lorelle moved to the side so she could see the new arrival.

"This is Max," Mal Ton muttered. "He's also Daniel Keller, Chancellor Howyn's pet mutant."

Anger surged through Lorelle and she came out from behind Mal Ton. He reached for her upper arm, but she jerked away. "Where the fuck is my sister?"

"I don't know." Max punctuated the statement with a smug smile and Lorelle snapped. She flew at him, but Mal Ton brought her up short. He encircled her waist with one arm and her chest with the other, trapping her hands against her sides.

"Let me go!" She kicked out with furious intent, but Max remained just out of reach. Slamming the back of her head into Mal Ton's chest, she shouted, "Where is she? Where is Brianna?"

"I really don't know." He looked around the room, his concerned stare belying his calm expression. "Did you kill my guards?"

"Senseless murder is your game, not ours," Fane snapped.

Why are we just standing here? Lorelle trembled with impotent rage.

Sweetheart, he can teleport offworld. If you get close enough to touch him, he'll take you with him. That's what he did to Andrea. This isn't the time or the place for a confrontation.

"You've lost the advantage of anonymity." Fane moved toward Max, drawing his attention away from Lorelle. "And you no longer have the chancellor's support. Whatever shall you do?"

Fane's jibe must have struck a nerve. Max's face flushed and his nostrils flared. "Don't even pretend this is over. I might have lost this round, but the fight has just begun." He flashed out of sight as suddenly as he'd flashed in.

Lorelle jerked against Mal Ton's restraining hands until he let her go. "He blithely tells you he knows nothing, so you just let him go?" She looked around for something to smash, anything. There had to be a way to relieve her seething frustration.

"We didn't *let* him do anything," Fane defended. "We just kept you from becoming his next victim. I lost two of my best men when we rescued Andrea. We will deal with Max, but he was not this mission's objective."

Her hands trembled as she finger combed her hair back from her face. They weren't afraid to fight. She'd seen them in action. "Do you believe him? How could he not know where Brianna is?"

"His mental shields are almost as powerful as mine," Mal Ton caught her hand and pulled her back into a light embrace. "When he said he didn't know where she was I sensed a spike of anger that nearly drove me backward."

"Then someone stole them out from under him?"

"My bet's on Howyn," Fane said. "Howyn knows more about the virus than anyone. He'll give Brianna the counteragent and—"

"Don't patronize me! Howyn's the one who kidnapped us in the first place. She's still in real danger."

"I was just trying to find a glimmer of light in the situation." Fane's charming smile failed to penetrate her aggravation.

"I appreciate the effort, but I'd rather have your anger and determination."

"They never waver." Mal Ton drew her attention away from Fane. "We will take down Howyn and Max because we won't stop trying until we do."

Fane started for the door with Mal Ton and Lorelle a step behind. "Today wasn't a complete loss. Two more humans are safe and not only is Max unmasked, he's obviously in trouble. There is no way he can take on Howyn and the Underground."

"Someone needs to tell Max. That was one smug son of a bitch." She accepted the outcome with a heavy sigh. "Retreat and fight another day?"

"This isn't a retreat," Fane objected. "Our mission was to rescue the women being held here and our mission was a success."

* * * * *

"If you don't stop sulking, I'll have no choice but to punish you." Mal Ton wrapped his arms around Lorelle's waist and pressed against her back. She'd barely said a word as they returned to the Underground. "Things aren't happening as fast as you'd like, but we're moving in the right direction."

"I know, but Brianna's my sister. I can't help worrying about her."

He turned her to face him and met her troubled gaze. "We'll get her back."

"Because we won't stop trying until we do?"

"Exactly." Her lips beckoned, but he wouldn't kiss her while her mood was still so volatile. "With Max on the run we can focus our efforts on Howyn."

"Why do you consider Max on the run? Long-range teleportation is a pretty daunting ability."

"Without Howyn's support Max can't win against Fane. We'll find a way to either control or contain him, but it will take planning and patience."

"It sounded like you and Fane have been suspicious of him for quite a while. Why haven't you moved against him before?"

"Daniel Keller was Howyn's puppet. He did nothing without the chancellor's permission. We saw a greater benefit in going after the man behind the mask. We suspected Keller might be Max, but we couldn't prove it until today."

"I still don't understand why Max shot down our ship. What was he hoping to gain?"

"A bargaining position with a much stronger opponent."

"Do you mean Howyn or Fane?"

"Howyn wanted your group badly enough to kidnap you. Max wants control of the Underground. We think Max intended to offer you and the other captives to Howyn in exchange for support as Max moved against Fane."

"And Howyn wants to incorporate our longevity into his superbeings?"

"That's Andrea's theory and it makes sense."

Lorelle nodded and moved closer, resting her head on his shoulder. "Howyn's ambition should buy us some time. He obviously wanted us alive or he would have killed us back on Earth. Bodies are a whole lot easier to transport than hostages."

"That's the spirit." His hands swept up and down her back as she sorted through her thoughts.

"Has Andrea figured out how I triggered bonding fever?"

"She's working on it."

With a soft chuckle, she raised her head. "It will just take time?"

He smiled and pushed his hands into her hair. "Not your favorite answer?"

"You've had centuries to learn patience. I'm just getting started."

"Sometimes I feel like I've become too patient. Your enthusiasm is wonderful."

"We balance each other?"

"In more ways than you realize." He brushed his thumb across her lips and savored the tingling heat cascading through his body.

"If everything else is beyond our control, I guess we have no choice but to finish all the things Amadi made us start."

"You'll get no argument from me." His mouth covered hers as his hands framed her face. Her lips parted and her mind opened. Longing washed over him in tantalizing waves. She wanted him, needed him, as badly as he needed her.

Their tongues slid against each other as their bodies aligned. He held her tight and she pressed even closer.

"I want you naked — now." Need filled her tone, not command, so he happily obliged.

Pulling his shirt over his head, he tossed it aside. He tugged off his boots while she attacked the fastenings at the front of his pants. Her eagerness thrilled him, speeding his pulse and hardening his cock.

She tugged off his boots and pushed down his pants before he could manage the task himself. He lifted his legs free, standing before her naked, tense with anticipation. He guided her hand to his erection. Her fingers curved around him and the smoldering embers of desire burst into consuming flames.

"Just the sight of you makes me ache all over," she whispered.

"I know the feeling. Or I will as soon as we get you out of these."

With the same frantic urgency, they rid her of her clothing. He reached for her breast, but she slipped to her knees with a siren's smile. "I'm pretty sure *this* is where we left off."

"I know I brag about my control, but I'm not sure I can take this tonight."

"Then don't resist. Revel in the pleasure." Her gaze liquefied with the last suggestion and she bent toward his cock.

Mal Ton clenched his fists as her agile tongue played over his engorged flesh. Desire pulsed across their private link, her excitement mingling with his. She kissed the very tip almost reverently then lifted him so she could reach the underside.

Each brush of her tongue drove his arousal higher. "Lorelle, I can't..."

"I know." Her warm breath teased his damp skin and he shivered. "I want to watch you and feel you and taste you."

He trembled, amazed at how easily she shattered his defenses. Unclenching his hands, he framed her face and pushed into her mouth. She met his gaze, her hands busy between his legs. Her fingers explored, touching and rolling, cupping and caressing until he feared for his sanity.

She moved her legs apart, never ceasing the sweet rhythm of her mouth. One of her hands descended with obvious purpose and he groaned. He wasn't sure why watching her touch herself sent his senses soaring, but it was undeniably arousing.

Her fingers moved in and out of her pussy for only a moment. He caught a glimpse of her cream shining on her skin then felt her fingertips circling his anus. She didn't mean to... With slow, firm pressure, she breached the tight collar of muscle and slid inside him. His cock bucked against her tongue and his balls tingled.

"You little devil." Through sheer force of will he fought back his release and enjoyed the bold slide of her slippery finger. Her tongue swirled around the tip of his cock at the beginning of each stroke. Firm and warm, her lips moved up and down the length of his shaft, her finger echoing the rhythm.

Come for me. I need you to let go.

Her softly coxing voice was more than he could withstand. Pleasure surged through him and swept into her. He pushed to the back of her mouth and released his seed down her throat. Shudder after heated shudder assailed his composure. He dropped his head back on his shoulders and moaned.

Lorelle watched Mal Ton come, thrilled by his momentary vulnerability as much as the sensations blasting across their link. His warrior's body trembled and pleasure contorted his features as he abandoned himself entirely.

He recovered by degrees. She caressed his legs and squeezed his ass, knowing he would soon deprive her of the pleasure. With a final shiver, he pulled out of her mouth and sighed.

"That was rather foolish." His brow arched as he pulled her to her feet. "Now my control is restored and you are at my mercy."

"There's no place I'd rather be."

Undeterred by the taste of his own passion, he kissed her long and hard. "Do you mean that?" He pulled back just far enough to look into her eyes.

"I don't understand what half of this means, but I know I've never felt like this before. I think I'm falling in love with you." He kissed her again, his mouth hungry and demanding.

I never thought… I never dared to dream this could happen to me.

She wasn't sure if he was uncomfortable saying it out loud or if he wasn't willing to stop kissing her long enough to speak. He hadn't actually said he loved her too, but his emotions were there in her mind.

Of course I love you. Never doubt it.

Joy bubbled up within her. It didn't matter that the last phrase had sounded a bit too commanding. He was her bonded mate, her lover, her protector and—her Master. Knowing the security and affection awaiting her within the role, she was no longer afraid.

His kiss drifted to her ear and descended along the side of her neck. She stroked his back and rubbed against him, lost in the perfection of the moment. His mouth was warm, his hands strong and sure.

Tenderness flowed into her from the most intimidating man she'd ever met. Each gentle touch was all the more precious because of his ferocity. He bent her back over his arm so he could reach her breasts. She relaxed in his embrace, trusting his strength and needing his passion.

His mouth teased her nipples, suckling with long, firm pulls. She arched into the caress and touched his face. Once her nipples were hard, moist peaks, he worked his way back to her mouth. "It's your turn to lose control, sweetheart. Are you ready to surrender?"

Chapter Eleven

ಐ

Lorelle stared into Mal Ton's eyes, reveling in the stark intensity. "I am yours as you are mine. I surrender willingly."

With a predatory growl, he swept her up in his arms and placed her on the bed. "Show me."

She raised her arms above her head and bent her knees. Her legs angled outward, parting her thighs and offering him her pussy. "Anything you want," she whispered, feeling breathless and strangely agitated. She wanted his cock inside her, filling the empty ache, yet the possessive gleam in his eyes warned her that actual penetration was a long way off.

He knelt between her thighs and touched her nipple. "You are so beautiful." His other hand traced her moist slit, pausing to circle her entrance. "All of you. You do not have permission to touch me, but I want you to come."

Accepting his words with a nod, she clutched the bedspread with her hands and watched his head descend. He licked her slowly, savoring her heat and her softness. She felt his enjoyment as well as her own. Her head spun at the combined pleasure.

His thumbs held her open and his fingers pressed against her bottom. He lavished attention on her clit, circling the puffy little bud until her belly jumped and her thighs trembled. Tension gathered within her, drawing tighter with each tantalizing pass.

"Too soon, I think." He raised his head and she whimpered. "We've got all night to play."

"I hate it when you get like this." She tried to relax, to disperse the tension he'd so skillfully built.

"You just said you loved me and you'd do anything I asked."

She licked her lips and pushed up on her elbows. "Are you going to make me regret my vow already?"

"Absolutely not." With their gazes locked, he pushed into her creamy core with two fingers.

She blew out a shaky breath and watched. Slow and steady he pumped into her body, her essence shining on his skin.

"You are so soft," he whispered.

His gaze fixed on her pussy and his cheeks were deeply flushed. Desire shined in his gaze and he licked his lips. Mesmerized by the savage beauty of his features, she focused on his eyes. The emotions she sensed in his mind were all there in his shimmering gaze. Desire, affection, anticipation and an intoxicating sense of wonder.

He buried his fingers in her cunt and brushed his thumb across her clit. The fingers inside her curved, rubbing the front wall of her passage. Pleasure swelled, ballooning out from the tips of his fingers. He plucked on her clit with his free hand, launching the sensation up through her body. She cried out and canted her hips as euphoria washed over her in waves.

Before she could fully recover, he slowly withdrew his fingers. "Turn over."

She'd all but dared him to push their boundaries. That didn't keep her heart from pounding. "Are you going to...?"

"We'll never do anything you're not ready to do."

With a tentative smile, she turned over and drew her legs beneath her. He rotated her so she was sideways across the bed and pulled her toward the edge of the mattress. She took a deep breath, allowing her desire to sweep aside her uncertainty. He would never hurt her. He had earned her trust over and over. She moved her legs apart and lowered her shoulders, resting her forehead on her folded arms.

He caressed her hips and squeezed her bottom, his thumbs dipping into the crack between her cheeks. She heard him pull open the nightstand, but kept her head down. Anticipation curled through her, rekindling hunger only partially sated by her recent orgasm.

"I know I brought this on myself," she whispered. Her pussy ached and her breasts felt swollen. "But I'm not sure I can take this tonight."

"'I want to watch you and feel you and taste you.' Wasn't that your response to my objections?"

"I'm a terrible tease," she murmured.

"No you're not." He placed one hand on the small of her back and eased the other between her thighs. "You're passionate and selfless, warm and responsive." As if to prove his claim, he drove a finger back into her feminine core.

She moaned, helplessly lifting her hips to take him deeper.

"Does that feel good?" He slid in and out while his other hand wandered over her upturned ass.

"Not nearly as good as your cock will feel."

"You'll have it soon enough." He withdrew his finger and her inner muscles fluttered. She wanted him there, needed his heat and his fullness. Using their link, she showed him the urgency of her desire. His breath hissed out and he squeezed her bottom with both hands. "We can always play after."

Allowing herself a pleased smile, she waited for the forceful thrust of his cock. Instead he parted her ass cheeks and gently inserted something small and smooth. Cool gel gushed into her rear passage and she shivered.

She wasn't sure what he intended, which only heightened the pleasure. Trusting him freed her to revel in the sensations. Something larger nudged her anus, teasing the sensitive opening with a circular caress. It didn't feel like flesh, more likely a toy of some sort.

"Relax, love. This is bigger than my fingers."

His other hand played over her folds, encouraging her as he pushed the toy into her untrained body. Pressure expanded like a swelling wave then her sphincter surrendered and the toy slipped inside.

"Your body will eventually take my cock, but we'll have to work up to it." He gently rolled her clit while he slid the toy in and out. "Tell me what you're feeling." She started to pass the sensations into his mind. "No. I want to hear you express how this makes you feel."

"I feel like my whole body is rushing out when you pull back."

"And when I push in?"

She concentrated on the sensations for a moment before she replied. "I feel more...invaded than when you're in my pussy."

His finger circled her clit, giving the pleasure an epicenter from which to expand. Each out stroke drew tingles along her tight passage and each inward thrust pushed them up her spine. She licked her lips and let him navigate the uncharted territory.

Suddenly he withdrew the toy and she looked back at him. "Why did you stop?"

With a sexy grin, he said, "I can't wait any longer." He tossed the dildo aside and picked up a tapered butt plug. The rounded end pressed against her slippery opening then she felt a moment of stunning pressure. Her body adjusted, contouring to the shape and holding it snug inside her. "All right?"

She nodded. The fullness felt odd yet not uncomfortable. He moved her to her side and then her back, his expression ravenous. He straddled one of her thighs and draped the other over his arm as he positioned himself against her vaginal opening.

He looked into her eyes as he drove into her core. The additional fullness accented his massive length. Deeper and

172

deeper he pushed. She raised one hand to stroke his face, but he warned her back with a soft growl. He paused and pulled her leg higher, resting her ankle on his shoulder. Her thighs were spread wide, her pelvis slightly turned.

A moment passed as they stared into each others eyes, savoring the long awaited joining. He pulled back slowly then thrust in fast. She concentrated on the thick slide of his cock and the intensity of his gaze. He held her, took her and possessed her. Each forceful thrust drove them higher, his passion feeding hers. She tightened herself around him, wanting to touch him yet unwilling to risk his displeasure.

"Touch me," he whispered, and she didn't hesitate.

She ran her hands up his arms, marveling at the rock-hard muscles beneath his smooth skin. His chest heaved beneath her fingertips. She stroked his sides and dug her fingernails into his back. He filled her over and over, his gaze never leaving her face.

Pleasure clouded his eyes half a second before the sensations burst into her mind. She wrapped her arms around him and closed her eyes. Her cunt tightened in rhythmic climax as he released his seed deep inside her.

Easing her leg down from his shoulder, he rolled them to their sides. He feathered kisses over her features as they basked in the afterglow.

"Do we just leave it in?" she whispered against his lips.

"Give me a few minutes and you won't mind it being there."

She smiled then hugged him close, hiding her face against his hair. "I wasn't talking about your cock. It is welcome to stay."

"Ah, the other." He ran his fingers down her spine and into the crack between her ass cheeks. "I can't quite reach it."

"Well, I don't want it out enough to separate. I guess it stays in for a while longer."

With tender kisses and evocative caresses he made her forget everything but the pleasure they shared.

* * * * *

"Andrea has been trying to figure out how you triggered bonding fever in Mal Ton," Fane told Lorelle the following afternoon. "As we suspected, she found Mal Ton's nanites in all of your samples."

Lorelle moved closer to Fane's desk, anxious to hear what he'd learned yet nonplused by the concern in his eyes. "Is this a problem? Mal Ton said his nanites aren't harmful."

Mal Ton slipped his arm around her waist and pulled her against his side. His gaze moved from her to Fane and back, but he remained quiet.

"They aren't harmful—to a Stilox." Fane rested his forearms on the desktop as he went on. "The virus made your DNA unstable and the nanites have been attempting to repair the damage ever since."

"But his nanites are programmed for Stilox physiology."

Fane nodded. "Andrea originally thought the changes in your DNA were due to how close you came to turning feral. Now she's nearly certain the nanites are responsible."

"Nearly certain?" She didn't like the sound of that. "What does this have to do with bonding fever?"

"The nanites are shaping your DNA according to the pattern they were given of optimum health. That pattern was Stilox, so their alterations have made you compatible with Mal Ton."

"Am I still human?" A long pause followed and tension wound around Lorelle like a ruthless constrictor. "Will these nanites continue to reshape my DNA until I'm fully Stilox?"

"We have no way of knowing," Fane admitted. "No one has ever seen anything like it before. But nanites aren't Andrea's field of expertise."

Lorelle looked at Mal Ton. "Who designed your nanites?"

"The design team is long dead. The only nanobiologists left are Protarian."

"Wonderful. The virus didn't get me but the nanites might? I love this world!"

"It's not as bad as I've made it sound." Compassion burned through the worry in Fane's gaze and he managed a weak smile. "The changes they've made so far appear to be stable and beneficial. Without these nanites, Mal Ton and I would have died long ago."

His casual revelation caught her attention. "You have nanites too?"

Fane averted his face as he admitted, "We were part of the same project." Someone pounded on the office door, preempting the rest of their conversation. "Come in."

The door burst open and a man in a military uniform was thrust into the room by an armed sentry. "I found him sniffing around outside."

"Thank you." Fane waited until the guard left before he addressed his uninvited guest. "What can I do for you, General Bryson?"

Tension was palpable and Lorelle reached for the small pulse pistol tucked into the back of her pants. Mal Ton touched her upper arm and shook his head.

Should we go?

Again he shook his head. *I suspect this will be interesting.*

"I've come on behalf of Chancellor Howyn." Bryson's voice sounded strained and he kept shifting his gaze between Mal Ton and Fane.

"Really?" Fane crossed is arms over his chest and leaned back in his chair. "What could Chancellor Howyn possibly want with me?"

"Doctor Myer was snatched from her apartment last night. We have strong indications that it was Daniel Keller."

"Offer the chancellor my condolences, but I fail to see what this has to do with me."

"The chancellor is willing to release the rest of the humans in exchange for Cassandra's safe return."

Lorelle's heart leapt into her throat and she could barely speak. "Who is Cassandra?"

"Howyn's daughter," Fane told her without shifting his gaze from Bryson. "He's the most powerful man on Protaria, why can't he find her himself?"

"You have resources at your disposal that Chancellor Howyn doesn't have."

Fane slammed his chair backward and stood. "This is rich. The only use he has for mutants is the abilities he can glean from our DNA. But now his daughter's life is on the line and he expects us to play hero?"

"In exchange for the humans."

Lorelle saw rebellion in Fane's eyes, but he asked, "Do you have any idea where he took her?"

"If we did, we wouldn't need you," Bryson snapped. Then he straightened his jacket and calmed his expression. "The culprit can teleport. The entire thing was recorded by safety surveillance. He appeared out of nowhere, wrapped his arms around her and disappeared." Fane just stared at him for a long, strained moment. "If the humans aren't incentive enough, I've been authorized to offer this as well." He held out an alloy injector. "Consider it prepayment."

"What is it?"

He glanced at Lorelle before he explained. "The original counteragent is only partially effective in humans. This is a refined counteragent."

Even if he's telling the truth, how the hell did they formulate a counteragent this quickly? Mal Ton sent the thought to Fane, but Lorelle heard it as well.

If I get my hands on Howyn's daughter, I'm not sure I can guarantee her safe return.

We should probably play along long enough to find out what the injector contains.

He'll release Brianna! Lorelle cut in. *There's nothing to debate.*

Her impassioned statement made Fane smile. "Tell Chancellor Howyn I accept his generous offer." He snatched the injector out of the general's hand. "We'll need more of this."

"I'll see to it."

Silence hung in the air long after the general left.

"Can we trust Howyn to fulfill his end of the bargain?" Lorelle asked.

"Hell no!"

"Not a chance." Mal Ton's response overlapped Fane's.

"If Howyn has known where we were, why hasn't he made a move against us?" Fane stroked his chin, obviously distressed by the implications.

"He was too busy obliterating Stilox," Mal Ton muttered.

"You said it yourself. His research is based on the abilities created through mutation." Lorelle shivered. "He needs you."

"He's going to find us harder to control than lab rats." Despite his calm expression, Fane sounded stunned. "What could Max possibly want with Cassandra Myer?"

"I didn't know Howyn had a daughter." Mal Ton shrugged. "Does it really matter why he took her?"

"I suspect it does." Fane handed the injector to Lorelle. "Have Ostan analyze that. I don't trust anything about this." They followed Fane into the corridor. "I'm going to the data center."

Mal Ton nodded and turned in the opposite direction. Lorelle was half a step behind him.

"Maybe Howyn loves his daughter enough to —"

"We can't trust the chancellor," Mal Ton insisted. "We'll hunt down Max *and* find out where Howyn stashed your sister. If we find them both, this alleged exchange will be moot."

She blew out a shaky breath. "My stomach is tied in knots."

"I know Bryson better than you do. It's hard to take him seriously after everything he's pulled in the past."

They descended the stairs from the great hall and found Ostan in the clinic. With his usual efficiency, he placed a drop of the counteragent under a molecular scanner. "If you hadn't told me this had been refined, I would have thought it was the original counteragent. The differences are infinitesimal."

"Is there any indication that the original counteragent didn't completely bind the virus?"

"The first group was taken to the safe house yesterday. I only have current scans of Lorelle and the two you brought in last night."

"Which counteragent were Donna and Kylie given?"

"I'm not sure. I'll cross reference this with their samples."

"Is there anything in the new counteragent that could harm a human?" Lorelle struggled to remain focused on one subject as all the possibilities raced through her mind.

"I know very little about human physiology." Ostan stepped back from the scanner and shrugged. "As long as you're not in immediate danger, I strongly recommend having Andrea's input on this."

Mal Ton agreed and they left the clinic. "We could take the counteragent to Andrea ourselves. It would give you an opportunity to talk with her and having direct access to you might speed her progress."

Repeated exposure to the subway tunnels wasn't making them any more pleasant. Lorelle hurried along at Mal Ton's side, trying not to think about the various substances crunching and sliding beneath her feet.

"I don't want to go anywhere until Brianna is safe."

"Gathering intel takes time. Bryson didn't give us much to go on. We'll likely be back before the action starts."

Renée huddled next to Fane as they shared a workstation. Her hand resting on his thigh, she leaned forward, offering him a better view of her cleavage. Lorelle fought back a smile. As long as Renée left Mal Ton alone, she didn't care who the scheming brat pursued. Besides, Fane could handle her.

"You're not going to believe this." Fane pushed back from the desk and casually disentangled himself from Renée. "Cassandra's field of expertise is nanobiology." Renée started to stand, but he dismissed her with a curt "Thank you".

"Does Max have nanites?" Lorelle asked as they moved away from the clutter of workstations.

"Not that we know of," Fane replied.

Instead of entering the tunnel, Fane led them through the dilapidated lobby and out of the building through a service door. The alley wasn't much better than the subway tunnel, but at least she could see the sky.

"Her occupation could have nothing to do with the kidnapping," Mal Ton said. "She's Howyn's daughter. Does Max need any other motivation?"

"No, but this is one hell of a motivation for us to recover her. If the chancellor is combining genetic manipulation with nanites, we need to know about it."

"And you think his daughter is going to brief you on their progress?" Mal Ton chuckled. "Good luck with that."

"Anything she knows I can learn." Mutant light flashed in Fane's gaze, making his harsh expression savage.

"As long as you're okay with scrambling her brain."

"It won't come to that. I have other tools at my disposal." Fane squared his shoulders and walked out of the alley. The street beyond was only slightly less neglected.

Lorelle had to rush to keep pace with the men. Mal Ton was focused on his longtime friend.

"You make this personal and it will only—"

"This is personal. It has always been personal. We've been on the defensive for far too long. If Howyn knows where we are there is no longer a reason to remain in the shadows." He glanced at Mal Ton and asked, "What did Ostan say about the counteragent?"

"He wants Andrea to analyze it. I was thinking about taking it to her myself, but the gleam in your eyes is making me nervous."

Fane waved away his concern. "Nothing is as stimulating as narrowly escaping death. We didn't go looking for this opportunity, but I'm not willing to waste it. That's all there is to my enthusiasm."

Mal Ton nodded, but he didn't look convinced.

"Go to Stilox. It's a good idea. Then Andrea can examine Lorelle and Lorelle can have her long-awaited conversation."

"Promise me you won't do anything rash until I return."

"You'll have to define rash."

"Agreeing not to terrorize Cassandra Myer would be a good start."

"You'll have to define terrorize." Fane winked at Lorelle. "Your mate is turning into an old woman."

She smiled. "He might be old, but he's very much a man."

"I'll take your word for it."

* * * * *

Lorelle watched Protaria shrink on the main viewscreen, torn between frustration and excitement. They had accomplished so much, yet even more remained unsettled.

"It's beautiful," she said, her tone hushed and distracted. Vivid blue oceans, gray-green land masses and swirls of fluffy white clouds. Protaria didn't look all that different from Earth.

He turned his chair and faced her, a sexy smile bowing his lips. "I'll take this view any day."

"You're certainly welcome to look."

His long fingers closed around her hand for a moment then drifted up her arm and cupped the side of her face. "I know everything has happened really fast for us. How are you holding up?"

"I want to know Brianna is safe, obviously, but the rest just feels…right." She covered his hand with hers and smiled into his eyes. "*You* feel right."

"You're certainly welcome to feel." He licked his lips and leaned toward her. "If we focus our efforts, we should have just enough time."

"Enough time for what?" she asked with a playful smile.

He nipped her bottom lip and unfastened his safety restraints. "I'll show you." The space between their seats was minimal so he turned her chair around and stood in the main aisle where there was more room.

She released the buckle securing her restraints and the straps separated with a clatter. He tugged her shirt and undergarment up, baring her breasts with one urgent motion. "If I had my way you'd never wear clothes. We spend too much time undressing."

"We don't have to undress. Just expose the important parts." Her fingers worked the fastenings on the front of his pants with the same hurried movements. She freed his cock and slipped to her knees before he could object to her boldness.

"I love the way you think," he whispered as she took him into her mouth.

Excitement stirred, speeding her pulse and firing her blood. She adored him with her tongue, savoring the heat and satiny softness. Her fingers grasped his thick shaft and pumped him to full erection. She would never tire of the raw power she sensed when she touched him or the tenderness it triggered inside her.

"My turn." The words sounded harsh and throaty as he pulled her to her feet.

Her chair had pivoted to face the console and he positioned her against the high, padded back. Liquid desire cascaded through her abdomen and gathered in her pussy. He unfastened her pants and pushed them to mid-thigh.

He didn't need to say a word. Emotions flowed freely across their link. Her desire fueled his and his heightened hers. Kneeling in front of her, he grasped her bottom with both hands and found her clit with his tongue.

She arched her back and rotated her hips, needing more than the teasing caress. Her legs were hampered by her pants. She tried to push them farther down, but he ignored her struggles and focused entirely on her sensitive nub.

With soft, coaxing swirls, he built her arousal. Her core melted and throbbed, needing his fullness and fervor.

"Please," she murmured.

He stood and turned her to face the chair. Dragging her pants lower with the toe of his boot, he eased his hand between her thighs and stroked her folds. "You're so wet." He pushed two fingers into her pussy. "Is all this for me?"

"Only you."

Reaching around her hip, he found her clit with his other hand. "Come for me."

He thrust into her with his fingers while he gently rolled her clit. She arched her back and rocked up onto the balls of her feet. Almost immediately, her core contracted and tingling heat spread through her abdomen.

"You'll have to do better than that." Working his slick fingers up to her other opening, he coated her anus with her cream.

Lorelle clutched the seatback, trembling with anticipation and need. His finger pushed past her sphincter and she gasped. Sensations rolled up her spine then dropped into the pit of her stomach.

Slowly he drew his finger back then pushed in deep. His other hand continued to work her sensitive bud. Her pussy rippled and her nipples tingled, another orgasm building between her thighs.

"That's right," he whispered into her ear. "Give it to me."

She rested her head against his shoulder and closed her eyes.

Lorelle's orgasm shook Mal Ton. The pleasure was so intense, his knees nearly buckled. She responded so sweetly and offered herself without reservation. He was humbled by her trust and determined to satisfy her completely.

He pulled his finger out of her tight rear passage and smiled at her moan. It thrilled him that she was willing to experiment, to explore the full range of carnal pleasures. He bent his knees and found her pussy with his cock.

She was hot and wet, beckoning him inward, and still he hesitated. As soon as he started moving inside her he wouldn't last long. Despite years of discipline she always managed to shatter his control. Unable to resist her heat, he pushed the head of his cock inside.

Wiggling restlessly, she pushed back against him.

"What's the matter?" he whispered into her ear.

"I want all of you."

"All of me?" he challenged. "What about my temper?"

"Yes."

He pushed in a little more, rewarding her with his fullness. "And my selfishness?"

"You're not selfish, you're focused."

He laughed and drove deeper. "Is that so?"

"More," she pleaded.

Refusing to be rushed, he held her waist and completed the penetration in one smooth drive. "How's that?"

"Better." She sighed and relaxed against the seat.

"Don't get too comfortable." He pulled back then thrust his full length into her snug passage.

Her inner muscles embraced him and his control snapped. With long, steady strokes he filled her body and caressed her mind. They moved as one, lost in the moment and the pleasure awaiting them. Harder and faster they climbed. Their cries echoed and their bodies strained. The summit rushed up to meet them and they dove headlong into release.

Also by Aubrey Ross

ಎಲ

E-Books:
A Taste of Dawn
A Taste of Midnight
A Taste of Oblivion
A Taste of Twilight
Crimson Awakening
Crimson Prey
Crimson Thrall
Dream Warriors
Ellora's Cavemen: Flavors of Ecstasy IV (*anthology*)
Seducer
Specter
Sorcerer
Soul Kisses
Velvet Deception

Print Books:
Candy Cravings (*anthology*)
Ellora's Cavemen: Flavors of Ecstasy IV (*anthology*)
Seducer

About the Author

෴

Aubrey Ross writes an eclectic assortment of erotic fiction. From power struggles between futuristic clans, to adventurous mystic guardians, her stories are filled with passion and imagination. Some of her recent awards include an EPPIE finalist, two Passionate Plume finalists, and a CAPA Nomination from the Romance Studio.

With a pampered cat curled on the corner of her desk, Aubrey dreams up fascinating words and larger than life adventures—and wouldn't have it any other way!

Aubrey welcomes comments from readers. You can find her website and email address on her author bio page at www.ellorascave.com.

Tell Us What You Think

We appreciate hearing reader opinions about our books. You can email us at Comments@EllorasCave.com.

Why an electronic book?

We live in the Information Age — an exciting time in the history of human civilization, in which technology rules supreme and continues to progress in leaps and bounds every minute of every day. For a multitude of reasons, more and more avid literary fans are opting to purchase e-books instead of paper books. The question from those not yet initiated into the world of electronic reading is simply: *Why?*

1. ***Price.*** An electronic title at Ellora's Cave Publishing and Cerridwen Press runs anywhere from 40% to 75% less than the cover price of the exact same title in paperback format. Why? Basic mathematics and cost. It is less expensive to publish an e-book (no paper and printing, no warehousing and shipping) than it is to publish a paperback, so the savings are passed along to the consumer.

2. ***Space.*** Running out of room in your house for your books? That is one worry you will never have with electronic books. For a low one-time cost, you can purchase a handheld device specifically designed for e-reading. Many e-readers have large, convenient screens for viewing. Better yet, hundreds of titles can be stored within your new library — on a single microchip. There are a variety of e-readers from different manufacturers. You can also read e-books on your PC or laptop computer. (Please note that Ellora's Cave does not endorse any specific brands.

You can check our websites at www.ellorascave.com or www.cerridwenpress.com for information we make available to new consumers.)

3. *Mobility.* Because your new e-library consists of only a microchip within a small, easily transportable e-reader, your entire cache of books can be taken with you wherever you go.

4. *Personal Viewing Preferences.* Are the words you are currently reading too small? Too large? Too… ANNOYING? Paperback books cannot be modified according to personal preferences, but e-books can.

5. *Instant Gratification.* Is it the middle of the night and all the bookstores near you are closed? Are you tired of waiting days, sometimes weeks, for bookstores to ship the novels you bought? Ellora's Cave Publishing sells instantaneous downloads twenty-four hours a day, seven days a week, every day of the year. Our webstore is never closed. Our e-book delivery system is 100% automated, meaning your order is filled as soon as you pay for it.

Those are a few of the top reasons why electronic books are replacing paperbacks for many avid readers.

As always, Ellora's Cave and Cerridwen Press welcome your questions and comments. We invite you to email us at Comments@ellorascave.com or write to us directly at Ellora's Cave Publishing Inc., 1056 Home Avenue, Akron, OH 44310-3502.

COMING TO A BOOKSTORE NEAR YOU!

ELLORA'S CAVE

Bestselling Authors Tour

Cerridwen, the Celtic Goddess of wisdom, was the muse who brought inspiration to storytellers and those in the creative arts. Cerridwen Press encompasses the best and most innovative stories in all genres of today's fiction. Visit our site and discover the newest titles by talented authors who still get inspired - much like the ancient storytellers did, once upon a time.

CERRIDWEN PRESS

www.cerridwenpress.com